D1020283

Go

author and photographer of *the secret life of it girls*

words and photographs by
DAKOTA LANE
ダコタ レーン

Lolita

ginee seo books
atheneum books for young readers
new york london toronto sydney

atheneum books for young readers † an imprint of simon & schuster children's publishing division † 1230 avenue of the americas, new york, new york 10020 † this book is a work of fiction. any references to historical events, real people, or real locales are used fictitiously. other names, characters, places, and incidents are products of the author's imagination, and any resemblance to actual events or locales or persons, living or dead, is entirely coincidental. †

book design by michael mccartney † the text for this book is set in itc esprit. † manufactured in the united states of america † first edition † 10 9 8 7 6 5 4 3 2 1 † library of congress cataloging-in-publication data † lane, dakota. † gothic lolita / dakota lane. — 1st ed. † p. cm. † "ginee seo books." † summary: sixteen-year-olds chelsea and miya have a lot in common, from their love of blogging, loss of loved ones, and the shōnen rainbow warrior books, to nationalities, even though they are halfway across the world from each other. † isbn-13: 978-1-4169-1396-2 † isbn-10: 1-4169-1396-3 † [1. blogs—fiction. 2. grief—fiction. 3. family problems—fiction. 4. hollywood (los angeles, calif.)—fiction. 5. japan—fiction.] † i. title. † pz7.l231785go 2008 † [fic]—dc22 † 2008015390

for the spirits at yaddo (they know who they are)

for h.h. ogyen trinley dorje & his farm

for laurie & gillian <33333333333

for yoshitomo nara & his lonesome puppy!!!!!!!!!

Chelsea

PART ONE. LOS ANGELES.

1.

i have to ask you something.

do you ever wish you had someone (not the sky someone, but a real person) who could share your reality?

there would be nowhere you could go that this person couldn't go, down to the details of your last strange dream. you'd be in this game together, just you and the other person creating the entire world.

i had that once, almost perfectly. and i want to tell you about it, but do i start with my reality—or do i tell you about the dream?

i've been having this dream.

i go to sleep at night—and then every morning, just at that point between light and dark, when the room seems to be jumping with shadows and energy, i dream that i awaken.

i awaken with akio in the room.

akio is a transparent green boy with cat ears. i would call him my invisible playmate, but he was always visible to me when i was small. he disappeared when i was three or younger, but here he is, back again in my dream.

and in this dream, i run out after akio—and instead of my familiar block in los angeles, we're in a place with no houses, the air so warm and still, trees all around.

akio is racing ahead, and i'm following him into a magical forest. . . .

and in the forest, akio leads me back to my little brother, memphis, and in this dream, i'm allowed to finally hug him.

i can touch his cheeks, i can really see him again, and i'm looking at every pore of his skin and thinking this time it's real—but before i can talk to my brother, he's running, and i'm chasing him through the sun-splashed forest.

sometimes we play—all our old games—and sometimes

he hides and i can't find him. but always, i end up being tired, and even though i am already sleeping, i close my eyes within the dream and curl up on the forest floor and sleep.

and when i wake, real life seems dimmer than the dream.

even now, half the colors are washed out of the world.

it's early in the morning and i'm walking to school, first day of tenth grade. dressed in hot dark clothes.
as i walk, my heels beat a rhythm into the pavement: MIYA, MIYA, MIYA, MIYA.

miya—of course you're on my mind.
i need to talk to you, but i'm torn.
i need you to be more than a phantom girl.
i also need you to recede into the shadows even farther.
i almost wish you would disappear, but today i can't pretend you're just an internet friend.

i should turn around and go back home. get online and tell you all the things i should have told you years ago.

but fear keeps me moving ahead, an invisible hand pulling me alongside the city park, keeping me on this pointless track. as long as i don't talk to you, i can stay in this in-between world, watching life like it's a river—flowing just out of reach.

birds chirping, moms pushing babies, a rush of noisy kids surging past me. school's just ahead, across the boulevard, tucked in the shadow of the hollywood hills. hot day, already hazy, i want to melt beneath the yellow sky.

i try to shut off the sounds when i pass the kiddie playground; a ton of kids crawling all over, racing and screaming. their sounds squeeze my heart with longing. i press my face against the fence, force myself to look, to focus on any one of them. alone in the sandbox, a little girl digging with a plastic spoon. she's wearing a white sundress and she's burying the feet of a naked doll and her entire being is involved in what she's doing. she must feel my stare, because she looks up—and straight through me.

my petticoats and black dress cling like layers of hot black tar. the brooch at my neck tightens in the heat. i feel weak, and the whole world seems to be getting darker. if i were a dog, i would fall down to the ground and just howl with the pain. but i'm not a dog and i'm not a crazy person.

i gaze out at the spotless lawn stretching from the playground to the little patch of trees at the end of the park. beyond that, black sticks against the sky—sixty acres of burnt wasteland, even after all these years.

i find the break in the fence and cut across the playground, full-out running across the chartreuse lawn, the world a blur, until i slip into the woods.

where is my brother? i can feel him grabbing my hand, pulling me into the next game. . . .

moving deeper inside the woods, picking through the branch-strewn path, cursing the muddy patches, trying not to breathe the bitter scent of eucalyptus.

—a splash—

and my heart jumps—

keep moving—

past the murky pond—

sit on a rock in the gray and green woods, bracing myself for the emptiness. i press my fingertips against the trunk of the tree where i made memphis believe in the elephant. we would always hug the tree and then leave a stone at the base, to help release the little spirit that was trapped inside. there are hundreds of stones in the pile, never moved in all these years.

the ground is littered with chunks of charred wood. this little corner of the park was completely untouched by the fire—but the embers traveled. i grab a piece and use it like charcoal to scribble on a rock—

where r u?

† † †

i won't cry in this place where memphis and i would catch spiders and dad would carry me on his shoulders to pick the highest leaves when they turned the color of lemons in the strange autumns of this city.

i lean my head against the tree. a whole card deck of memories falls into my face: shopping for school supplies with mom, her nervous face when she waved good-bye from the window, the way i used to run home from school full of things to tell her—ancient, ancient scenes, little-kid scenes, all the way before memphis was born.

an ache at the back of my throat, just because this is the first time mom isn't home when i start school. she's in japan; when the phone rang around 1 a.m., i ran to get it—it had to be her—but it stopped ringing before i reached it. just as well—she's waiting for an answer i'm not ready to give.

there's a cool peppery smell in the air, in the shadows by the pond, so rich i can almost taste it; tiny gold bugs disappear like drops of mercury in the black moss at my knees. each beautiful thing hurts.

so hot. black sweat down my back, don't melt my dress.

i won't cry. like an idiot baby.

maybe mom's moving on, but i'm not ready to.

i feel the warmth rising, the ghosts of the forest steaming the air. it's been three years since memphis disappeared. tomorrow—september 2nd—it will be exactly the day.

i know he'll come back to me—i feel positive it's going to happen tomorrow. we'll be together again—right here in these woods.

it's time to head out, but i'm not going home, because how can i tell you any of this?

2.

you have probably built a picture of me in your mind out of the fragments i used to post on my blog.

do i wear color in your mind, or am i all in black?

when i was little, i craved color; memphis, too. it was our mother's fault—she got us addicted to a japanese manga about rainbow warriors. color had a life of its own—no matter how our mother tried to tone us down, colored rays would find us, stick to us, spill out of our drawers. even our rooms were painted in vibrant hues.

how did my world become so black?

3.

the skins of black snakes live on my floor, pieces of lolita
that i haven't ironed or hung back on satin hangers, pieces
of my past. i fish any of these pieces off the floor,
that's how i get dressed,
and this is what i'm wearing, this black dress,
and this is how i live, cloaked in dark sunshine,
between life and death, ready for my brother's return.

† † †

i'm out of the woods, walking fast
so i won't be late for school.
the hollywood hills are brownish lumps,
crouched in the distance.
in a moment, i will stop the world
and trace the image of your mountain
over the tired hills.
mt. fuji will appear.
ice will begin to run through my veins.
i will grow cool and strong enough for anything.

i have only you to thank for this.
at times you have been my only friend.
in return, i have given you nothing—
and that is part of my shame.
i know you've been trying to reach me.
when you discover that i've been here in the shadows, will you be able to forgive me?

for three years, i've kept you waiting—but you refuse to believe that our connection is dead. i never asked to have so much power over your fate, and i have this terrible feeling that if things were reversed, you would be so much kinder to me.

PART TWO. JAPAN.

1.

it's dinnertime and i can't eat. there's a bad feeling in the dining room and my bowl of noodles looks like worms.

was it only three nights ago? i was in my father's hospital room, and the tv was on—a reality marathon, nonstop episodes of *the lonely man*, most popular show in tokyo, about an old man who leads a dull and ordinary life. the camera stays on him while he does things like shave, read the paper, boil water for tea. it was basically all my father would look at.

around three a.m., my father fell asleep with the tv remote on his chest—just seconds after *the lonely man* had also nodded out in front of his tv. the whole show at this point was *the lonely man* softly snoring on his couch. all over japan, thousands of people had probably been waiting for this moment—i could feel a distinct shift in the atmosphere, as if my entire country had fallen asleep.

i was wide awake, watching the screen monitoring my father's heart. i saw the green peaks on the screen by his bed turn into a flat green line, as if all the mountains of his life had been wiped out with his last breath.

the machine made the exact noise that you hear in movies, when the line goes flat and the hero dies, and right about then, my own life became a sort of movie. my father was dead. things were happening around me but not quite touching me, and it kept going like that for a few days, until i sprang back to reality at my father's funeral today, and it hurt so much to be alive. i had a knife digging inside me, precise and sharp, tracing designs inside my gut as they lowered his coffin into the ground. i squeezed my little brother's hand so hard that i gave him a violet bruise.

i felt a presence then, like a touch on my shoulder—a warmth and peacefulness settled into me. just a simple comfort, and so familiar.

† † †

i'm sitting at the table now, for the evening meal, looking at the rules posted on the wall right next to the clock. i've been here for close to three years now, and no one's ever broken one.

it's getting dark outside. a cold silence—
there is no hunger inside me. the funeral was only a few hours ago—how can they eat?

† † †

he died at three a.m.
the sun was coming up by the time i got a ride home from the hospital, and i was thinking, here is a sunrise that dad won't see. we drove along the river; it was a quiet morning, even the early rush-hour traffic seemed sedate and orderly. i was thinking, i wonder if i will remember everything about this moment, this moment of my first day without my father in the world.

i crawled into bed with my brother, couldn't stand to be alone.

shut my eyes—and had just barely fallen asleep when a powerful force woke me, as if the room had been flooded with light and sound. but when i opened my eyes, all i could see was akio, standing at the door, with his serious face and furry cat ears, a green little boy, my imaginary playmate from childhood.

i started to follow him out the door, the way i used to when i was small—the dream was so realistic, i could feel the bare floor on my feet and i turned back and looked at the bed, and sure enough, my brother was still asleep, curled up with the plank of wood he likes to cuddle, his favorite toy—and i could see a first ray of sun hitting my brother's cheek—you can hardly imagine how vivid this dream was—and i followed the green catboy out the door, but when i stood at the threshold of the door, i wasn't looking out at kamakura, or even solid earth; below me and before me were acres and acres of rolling clouds, lit from beneath with a pink light, and if i took one more step, i would be flying.

warm currents beckoned me—all i had to do was step out and i would be leaving this depressing place and flying

toward home; there was this absolute feeling that if i made the choice, i could go home.
it was very clear: either walk through that door, or don't.

i awakened with a start, and the first thing on my mind was my brother. he never seemed to be part of the choice. in the dream, i didn't feel like i was leaving him behind—it was like the whole dream was focused on me. and it left me feeling guilty, even though it was just a dream. how could i forget my brother, even for a second, even in a dream?

i've had it three or four times—i've lost track of the days, because time is passing in a strange way now, speeded up or slowed down. i feel like i have slipped between the minutes since my father died.

my brother doesn't really get that our father is dead—he's not even three yet. and if he knew, it wouldn't make him scream. he only screams when he feels invaded—by things that wouldn't bother most people: light, sound, an unexpected touch. and then he yells like he's being tortured.

but he's settled now. catches my gaze, all serene and dreamy, sighing in contentment: he loves ramen. he's eating the noodles one at a time, delicately, with his fingers—until he grabs up a fistful, slurping them noisily, eyes gleaming like a demon.

soon the older kids start copying him, and next thing it's a big slurpfest. everyone goes back to eating as we have eaten every night, at this long, ugly table in this too-bright and too-hot room, as if my father hadn't been buried today. everyone relaxes.

everyone but the american.
she's here to adopt a kid, that's all i know. rumors always fly if you listen to the ladies who run this place, but i try not to. you hear too many sad and violent stories if you listen.
she catches my eye in that empathetic way she has, and a wave of hatred sweeps through me. sweat breaks out on my forehead, and i have to gulp down my whole glass of cold water or else i might throw it in her face. she has the baby, nanako, on her lap.

the baby was born only a week ago. i get a good look at her eyes: dreamy and unfocused; she doesn't seem like she's

landed in her body yet, and i don't blame her.
stay away as long as you can, nanako-chan!
her eyes flutter closed like she hears me.
then she lets out this little mew, and the american hoists her to her shoulder, murmuring and gently patting her.
i look at my brother. he flashes a smile at me—
he doesn't get how i used to carry him like that.
how heavy he was.
the way his eyes looked silver at night.
how he had fat cheeks just like this baby and a silky mohawk that you just wanted to spike up with gel. and the way we had a sort of communion.

† † †

at first i felt strange with this little being in my arms beaming out such pure love, when i held him late at night. he drank from his bottle, and the whole time he looked up into my eyes—it seemed with curiosity, like he didn't recognize me—but then i realized he was holding a constant gaze of love.

i'd never even held a baby, let alone fed one and had it stare at me—i wanted to look away—but we were alone, and i was

curious too. it was amazing that there was this new person here and he was my brother, so i relaxed, finally, and i'd look back at him for hours, with the same pure love.
he doesn't remember one thing about it, so what good was it? i'm starting to forget all the details myself.
and three years from now, he probably won't even remember that i'm the only human he will allow to touch him.

so beautiful, they say about my brother, drooling over his long lashes, his intense gaze, *so incredibly beautiful—like an anime, with that adorable grin, oh, aren't you precious*—and when they lean close, he punches them in the face. or spits. a backhand slap. maybe a bite.

like he bit the american a few days ago, only moments after she arrived. the american was first here a year ago, snooping around. good luck getting nanako—her parents are apparently both alive, and they'll never let her go. she'll probably stay here until she's fifty.

i don't even know why i hate the american so much.

but the moment she walked in, she scooped up the baby,

and the ladies actually let her stay in nanako's room to help out—diapers, bottles, etc., she said she didn't mind. so she was getting settled in her room, and my brother goes in to check her out and two seconds later—*chomp!* he bit her hand.

things like that are not supposed to make you feel a tender glow of pride. there is something wrong with me.

the american goes into the kitchen and comes back with some tea. she's good at carrying the baby and simultaneously doing other things. not a helpless type.

i caught a glimpse of how neat she was keeping the room—upstairs, across from the bathroom—*matsu's old room*, i always call it, even though she moved away ages ago.

in the hospital, i was shocked when dad blurted out, *whatever happened to that matsu girl?*

i feel a thud in my chest—*dad.*
it keeps happening: i forget—but only for a fraction of a second—and then the truth slams back into me, so hard

that i expect the people around me to be shaken by it too. no one warns anyone about this situation. they should be explaining it to you from the moment you're born, they should brand the idea into your head, they should tell us the truth about death.

how horrific and final it really feels—and how alone you will be with the horror. and how you will forget for just a second, and when you remember again, it's like remembering that the sun has been extinguished.

† † †

nothing, i told him, *nothing happened to matsu.* i was pissed; or maybe *jealous* is a better word. he didn't ask what had happened to me over the past two years, all he wanted to know is if i was still practicing my violin, because i guess he forgot that i left it out in the rain when i was twelve and that was that.

in the hospital, i could barely stand to see the way he was lying there so passively, looking so ready to be plucked out of this life.

† † †

when i was little, dad was my lifeline.
i would stand in the window
watching for him to come home.
he was my rock and my world.
i don't know if i can handle being like that for my brother.
orphans. the word makes a noose around my throat, but my brother's oblivious. the truth is, even if he understood, he wouldn't stop slurping one noodle.
all he's ever needed is me.
outside it's finally dark, a rich purple twilight that makes me want to bolt out of the house and lose myself in it.

† † †

maybe he was tired of the silence between us, tired of hearing nothing but the random coughs coming from *the lonely man.* but when dad asked me to read to him—even though he said it mildly, barely looking at me—i felt an urgency about it, looking around wildly for something to read. nothing, not even a newspaper. nothing, except for the manga i'd brought—so i opened it and began to read, imagining that the words were filling him with substance, anchoring him to earth.

i read in a kind of trance, and i could practically see them—the characters climbing out of the book and sitting on the edge of his bed; as i read, i prayed that they would take over where i had failed.

gothiclolita009 was born with such a deep sense of longing that she often wondered if she had come from another realm. . . .

i followed akio . . .

their time had run out.

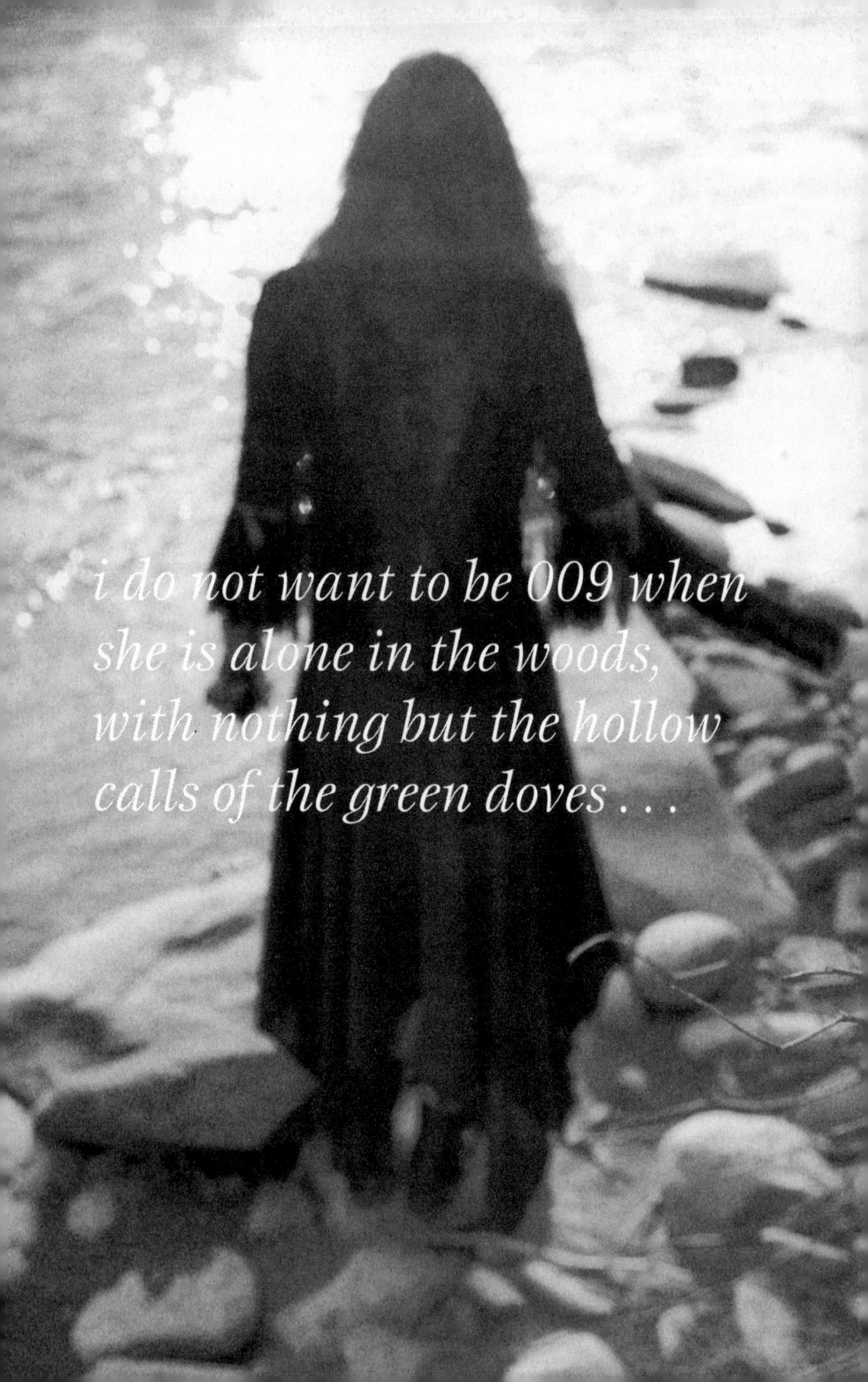
i do not want to be 009 when
she is alone in the woods,
with nothing but the hollow
calls of the green doves . . .

it was the first time i saw
a real gothic lolita.

2.

i remember the first time i saw this place—i had no clue it was an orphanage, although the sign in the front gave me the creeps—THE MORNINGSTAR FOUNDATION. for a second, it seemed possible that dad was taking us to a place where my brother and i would be experimented on—it was like something straight out of one of my mangas.

it looks like a normal house, my father said, almost to himself. it was the largest one on the hill, with a view of the train tracks running alongside the river. it was cold, and i was carrying my brother—i had him half inside my coat. dad said nothing to me—until it was finally time to say good-bye, and then he choked up and apologized. his head drooped. we hugged, and i thought he would be back to get us soon.

that was more than two and a half years ago, and no matter how normal this place looks on the outside, it's never felt like home.

gothiclolita009 felt frightened and alone—but in reality, there were whole tribes of children like her, millions of children, some of them abused and all of them abandoned—stashed away in unassuming institutions. society knew of their existence: the hidden children were a dark spot in the back of people's minds. all those who chose to ignore were guilty—and the guilty would soon be erased—at least that's what 009 liked to think when she was in an evil mood. . . .

that's how the first *shōnen rainbow warrior* book starts, and the plot gets deeper and more intense as it goes. pieces of the books automatically cling to my mind—it's not like i try to memorize it.

for millions of years, gothiclolita009 was a rainbow warrior and ruler of the crystal realm, along with her eternal love, shōnen. all is bliss—until she answers the call of a crying child and tumbles into the foul underworld of shadowland. she's forced into the form of a suffering human and seems doomed to remain for an eternity—

will shōnen help her to recall her true identity?
or will he fail and join her as a suffering human in shadowland, shattering the entire crystal realm? the basic premise of the whole six-book series never changes—but just

thinking about it makes me want to run upstairs and pull the books out from under the covers on my bed.

i completely identify with 009—
quirky observations, twisted humor, even the things she eats.
both of us without parents.
and both pulled out of sleep throughout our lives. the moon falls into our bedrooms and hits our closed eyes—and the little spirit appears, daring us to follow.
but unlike me, 009 escapes on those nights, throwing herself into the harsh action of tokyo:

. . . she drank down the essence of the city like a bitter medicine. she let it burn her throat and sear her organs, just to remind herself that she was alive, and when she was drunk beyond all reason, she left nihilistic graffiti in the bathroom of every karaoke bar. . . .

009 is never far from my mind, and even in the cemetery—as the clouds burned bright in the sky above our heads—i could see her burying her own father, beneath a sun blotted out by black crows.

3.

i don't like the way that american is looking at my brother. she's going on in singsongy baby talk to nanako. her japanese is flawless except for a tiny american accent. who knows why her voice hits my ears like someone eating glass.

she's humming to the baby, but she keeps peeking at my brother, throwing him smiles, like she's half singing to him. and he's looking back, actually being pulled in by it. a red streak runs through me: warning . . . jealousy—

but it's the baby he likes.

it's so cute the way he's been peeking at her like she's a fascinating new toy, ever since she arrived. i'm waiting for him to just dive in and grab her. he doesn't exactly honor boundaries.

earlier tonight, the american had her bag down here, and my brother just helped himself to her cell phone. maniacally pressing buttons, ended up auto-dialing some number in the u.s. the american took it well. *it's early in the morning there,* she told my brother, as if he cared. she examined the face of her phone, and she smiled. *he dialed my daughter's number,* she said to the room, or maybe to me, but i felt a sickening lurch and turned away, and all i could see was a spoiled american girl with her own phone, two parents, no worries.

the american had the grace to stop herself.

† † †

sixteen is supposed to be the cutoff point in this place: it doesn't matter if your father is dead or alive, you have to leave.

matsu was fifteen when she ran away; she never came back, but i went to see her once; we had this crazy time in tokyo.

no one's brought up the subject, but i know how it works: they'll kick me out or ship me to a larger institution in yokohama city—and there's a waiting list of hundreds ready to adopt an adorable japanese boy. they don't realize i would kill before i let this happen to my brother.
i turned sixteen back in june—so i'm already out of time.

† † †

the american was up early this morning, standing in the kitchen watching me make coffee.
if there's anything i can do . . . she was dressed immaculately for the funeral.
i wanted to say, *yeah, you can not be here.*
i was pissed that she was coming, treating it like some kind of plum blossom festival. but i forgot about her once we got to the cemetery. i never even noticed her there, until she came up and rested her hand on my brother's head. she had tears in her eyes as if she were a mourner. she actually tried to hug me—i caught that same pulling look in her eyes, right before i turned my back and walked out of her reach.

if i let her near me, she'll crack my head open and scoop out all my private thoughts. americans are so invasive some-times. (that's partly why i love them.)
—but i do need to get it all out, i can feel everything i want to say, all lodged in my throat, it would feel so good to just let it out. sometimes i wish i had a person to tell everything to, to just talk and talk. up all night, just laying it out.
but maybe it's not even words. if only you could be

somewhere so isolated that you could scream until there were no screams left inside you.
when my brother has one of his fits, part of me is jealous: when will i get a turn?

† † †

i run upstairs—leaving my brother, my plate of food—but no one stops me on this night.
i slam into my room and sit at my desk in front of my computer—to what?
dump everything into my blog, just let the truth fly out; you never know, tonight could be the night i let my feelings spill—
i actually call up my page, take a deep breath, and—
can't even start.

too much inside that's not ready to be disguised in normal words. i always name my blogs. what would i name today's blog—*dad's dead*?
how about: *no way out.*
or just: *please help.*

so i go to lolichan16's page, like i do every day.
she would never let me drown.
she'd try and pull me out of this,
in her own lolichan16 way, if only she knew
what i was going through.
i catch her icon flashing on my page sometimes, so at least i
know two things: she's alive. and she still reads me.

but her last blog was almost three years ago.

i'm just checking.
again.
to see if she's come back.
—how many times do i do this?
sometimes twice a day.
obsessive.
pitiful.

press my fingertips into my eyes, calling to someone.
there must be so many of us whispering for help tonight.
but i can feel someone on the other side, listening.
is it *you*?

4.

i've felt you always—even though grandma didn't tell me about you until i was almost thirteen.

your mom always has difficult pregnancies, she said. we were in her garden, and she was vigorously raking the beds. my mother was in bed, sick and pregnant with my brother. we lived next door to grandma.
my grandmother stared into me, as if she were reading something printed on the inside of my skull.
you might as well know, she said. *when your mom was pregnant with you, you weren't alone. she was supposed to have twins. at first there were two heartbeats—and then . . .* she nodded, as if that was it, i could figure out the rest.

and then, grandma? and then, ***what?***

and then there was one. one died so the other could live. your mom didn't want you to feel guilty.
but i did. guilt and that eerie sense of connection.
i'd been talking to you even before i had words.
no, i mean you really must not be guilty, miya. she took me by

the shoulders and pulled me close and trained her blackest black-sky eyes on me: *because she was born immediately to someone else.*

i felt a flash of coldness run down my arms and didn't dare ask for details. she nodded in agreement with herself, eyes never leaving mine.

twins run in this family, she said, almost as an afterthought, already back to raking—she didn't need to tell me not to repeat what i'd heard; when she told me things, i was never tempted to break the secret.

† † †

for years, you've been like a flickering shadow, but at the funeral, you were so close, i felt if i turned quickly, i'd see you.

it was you, wasn't it?

i haven't felt your presence so strongly for such a long time.

where the heck have you been?

Chelsea

PART THREE. LOS ANGELES.

1.

i'm tasting snow, almost. the cold stings my eyes and i feel it at my nostrils; i've blurred out the hollywood hills, and over them i'm tracing a towering mountain—a frozen giant, flat at the top, larger than all the hills put together, an image from your life.

i have always taken pictures from your life and imagined them in place of my reality.

you have given me things i can hold on to.

when i saw the first photograph of mt. fuji that you posted—

taken on the beach—shimmering up behind your town, like a thin hallucination—i knew you would climb it.
and when i saw the other—extreme close-up of twigs

encased in sparkling ice—i knew you had made it at least partway up.
i could feel you kneeling, freezing, fumbling for the camera, holding your breath to get the sun shattering the ice into rainbows. . . .
all you wrote was: *went here today!*
two photos, three words.

you put only fragments on your blog, and i take those fragments out when i need to and stretch them over my world.
on the way to school. on the way home from school.
you put those pictures up so long ago, and i've conjured up mt. fuji so many times that now it appears all by itself. it's just a game, even though it doesn't always feel like play.

† † †

as close as we are, there's so little we know about each other. i realize i've left out a lot—but so have you.
but at least you keep writing. i haven't written a word to you since memphis disappeared.
you don't even know what happened.

† † †

i couldn't reveal the deepest truth in a blog. when i first did my blog, i could barely get two or three words out—never a real feeling—without hearing that random savage bitch:
say it faster.
funnier.
sharper.
wtf—emo poseur.
omg, that is so gay.

the random savage internet bitch, the one who exists inside everyone's head—she's the one who made me hide.

in reality, gangs of people weren't roaming around looking for blogs to trash. kids at my school were basically using the space as a message center—hardly anyone took the time to keep or read blogs. but when you're online, you can feel the hum of millions; you don't trick yourself into thinking you're curled up in bed with a cozy diary.

even if they weren't likely to peek inside my blog, i could *feel* them—an entire army of random savage bitches ready

to pounce if i exposed one inch of real flesh.
i began to choke out tiny pieces: a sentence, a link, a picture.
and in spite of my fear of being exposed in some way, i had only one reader: you.

and i had to go out and find you first.

i know there's a logical explanation for our connection. but there's also a magic. the way i found you started with the *shōnen rainbow warrior* books.

† † †

gothiclolita009 was the star of a japanese manga that my mother had been reading to me since i was born. 009 was the saddest and most beautiful girl in the world to me.

she had fallen from the crystal realm into the body of a street urchin. she lived in an orphanage and haunted the streets of an eerie japanese town—and the only place she found joy was in a forest. her true love, shōnen, would take the form of a human and meet her there, but their time together would soon be running out—unless he decided to stay and be human forever. . . .

my mother obviously loved the story, but her main concern was that i would learn japanese. she was born in japan but had come here as a young teen. she hoped that the language would seep painlessly into my head, because she wasn't the teacher type.

every year, as i understood more japanese, i began to understand more about the story. my mother had been giving me a book a year, starting with my fourth birthday, so by the time i was seven, i had the first four books of the series.

my mother wouldn't say where they came from, but there was a note scribbled in english on the end page of the last book: *if found, please return to*—and there was an address in a remote town in japan.

† † †

i was seven when i grabbed a magazine that someone left

on the kitchen table, only because the giant headline mentioned my hero:

GOTHIC LOLITA: CULT OR FASHION?
An Inside Look at the Famous Costumed Kids of Tokyo

i didn't normally nab things from the adult world, but i leafed through, heart pounding, expecting to see something about 009.

instead, eerie shots of teens—young women who looked like children forced to pose in victorian maids' outfits. puffed sleeves, black capes, lacy parasols, some with veils—they were elegant and dignified and darkly innocent. they looked like actors or models to me. like things i'd seen flashing by on tv.

but there were others—sitting on the ground like stranded orphans, clinging to baby dolls. their eyes flat and vacant.
i couldn't take my eyes off these *others.*
nothing about them seemed fake or costumed; suffering came off them in waves, and they had the faces of real children.

they looked exactly the way i'd imagined 009—*after* her fall.
they seemed like the scariest girls in the world.
(i didn't know that someday i would want to be like them.)

but when i turned the page, it was like moving into oz.
same scene, but different girls, some in alice-in-wonderland frocks, others in candy-colored costumes—wildly layered creations with plastic toys worn like necklaces—some with bunni ears, violet plaid knickers mixed with orange plastic shoes. . . .

one cluster of girls wore phosphorescent dresses; they caught the light in a most ethereal way, giving them the feel of holographs. in my mind, they looked like rainbow warriors.

i imagined myself posing with them, icy pastel shimmers of gloss on my lips and eyes and cheeks, skin polished with a sparkly dust of mild green and baby pink . . . no shoes on my feet, but toenails the color of pearls and seashells. i would be an intergalactic mermaid splashing into the hearts of the enthralled crowd, a cyberdelic creature.
i had no idea in those days what *gothic lolita* really meant.

to me, it was all about the character in my manga. it was all about being an ethereal being.
i basically just loved the sound of it: *gothic lolita.*
when i started my blog, i was eleven.
i wanted to find someone completely different from me.
and at the same time, i wanted to find someone exactly like me.
i was so curious about japan.
so i did a keyword search on girlbloggers.com: i put in *gothic lolita* and the postal code from the address in the back of the shōnen book—and viola!
yours was the only name that came up.
your page: stark and mysterious and beautiful—just as i hoped.
your name, just as beautiful: miya.
i never wrote to you and you never wrote to me.
but i read you.
you saw my little icon and you read me back.
i started with you—but i assumed that i would soon have many readers.

every day, the little girlblogger thingy would pop up and ask: *would you like to see who has been visiting your page today?*

—and your icon would come up each time.
i have to admit i felt safe that both of us had blocked all comments. but never safe enough to say what i really felt.
sometimes i would let my fingers fly—then delete it all without rereading. . . .
mostly, i would keep it all back, even from myself.
i would go on, and i could feel it rising within me, everything aching to the surface, and then i'd post only five or six words.
mood: oppressive.
love is so destructive.

i felt like i had a hidden safe inside me where every ugly secret was automatically filed, sometimes so quickly that i didn't even have time to take a look at it myself.

† † †

what if i were to tell you that when i was little, i used to walk looking at the ground, so i wouldn't have to meet human eyes?

those foolish enough to look into 009's mournful eyes would fall prey to her terrible spell, instantly becoming soldiers in the army of sorrow. . . .

my mother was walking me home from school—just ahead of me, talking to another mother. i was looking at the ground, at the leaves. i had a way of looking at things with half-closed eyes, to blur them, because the world was easier if you couldn't see anything too clearly.

the leaves were strewn all over the sidewalks of the decayed city—and as she stepped on them, she could hear the faintest voices from the other side . . . the voices of old friends, visiting from the crystal realm. . . .

sometimes i would read my book while i walked. if i walked with my head in a book, i could be in two worlds simultaneously, with the book world taking precedence. but this time i was just imagining myself inside the story.

i had to almost put myself into a trance to get there, but i was getting better at it; it was like falling down a dark but comforting tunnel, the blurred eyes, the leaf voice.

a new wave of kids was coming up behind, there were dozens leaving the school, so i imagined an invisible shield for my body and i concentrated harder on the ground, listening for instructions from the leaves—and there in the center of a dark cluster of leaves, i saw the golden eggs. . . .

i couldn't believe my luck at finding such treasure. i knelt down in the leaves and reached to touch them—their surface seemed almost transparent, not hard like a shell, but when i touched one, it wasn't what i expected. it was warm, on the verge of sticky, and even as my finger still poked it, i saw the shape all around it, half hidden in the black wet leaves, camouflaged, revealing itself to me as a dead, black-leaf-colored cat. i was kneeling on the sidewalk with my finger gently probing the guts of a dead cat. gross!

a loud scuffling of hard shoes in the leaves all around me. *gross,* they squealed, in a close circle around me. *she's touching a dead cat!*

i wasn't touching it anymore, but i was still kneeling before it, guilty.

remember that time you were playing with a dead cat? mariah asked me years later when we were drunk on top of her roof one night.
hell yeah, i said, like i had done it on purpose and liked the whole experience, because that's how i had stopped being a freak—i had restyled my past to match the new fake me.

you were such a gothic little creature. she propped up on an elbow and looked at me so admiringly, i felt a swoop in my heart. i grabbed the bottle from her hand and took the tiniest swig of her beer. she lived not far from the beach. there was a warm wetness to the night air, and i wanted to go out in it. this whole nostalgic yearning was stirring inside me.

i just wanted to leave her house and take a walk. i thought i could smell doughnuts, a sweet vanilla scent—maybe they were baking somewhere and we could get them. we could sit in a doughnut shop and spin on stools and make up stories about the people who stopped in. . . .

right. the kind of thing i'd do with mom. when i was six.

i almost told her everything, i almost explained myself—but it was easy to keep it in with mariah.

when i sat in front of my computer and didn't let the truth out, it took as much effort as if i were holding back a live monster.

but what if i let it escape now—

would you run?

PART FOUR. JAPAN.

1.

so what about this silver cross? i turn it in the light to catch the dull gleam.

it's not heavy enough, right? definitely not gothic. but i like the way it's so delicate. my grandmother gave it to me.

i've got a pretty good pile in the center of the room, but it's really hard for me to sort through things. at times like this, everything seems so important. i want to get out of here with as little as possible. but this cross, it carries the essence of my grandmother's little house—or at least i imagine when i breathe that i can still find the fragile scent of green pine incense and a touch of the burnt black smoke of frying cod. not as bad as it sounds. i put the cross in the center of the pile.

and her picture—of course i need that. the only one i

have—her square, crooked glasses, crooked because one of her ears was higher than the other. she died the same year as my mother, and luckily, i haven't seen either of them since.

i think i would freak if i had to actually see some relative's spirit; it wouldn't be charming or comforting like it was when i'd see my so-called invisible friend.

† † †

akio was green. he had cat ears and was shorter than me, and i didn't even think of him as being a spirit—to me, he was as real as my brother. and obviously not invisible—how could you not see someone who was green and had cat ears?

i can almost see him too, said my grandmother. *he was your father's imaginary playmate too. he loved him so much, he insisted he was always with him, far into his teens. we called it a* zashiki-warashi—*a little boy spirit. legend has it that once he's in a family, he never goes away. . . .*

i yelled at my mother when she sat on him while i was

taking my bath. (he was on the edge of the tub, exactly where she put her butt.)

when he was gone, i would get rocks in my stomach and talk to him through a seashell i kept under my pillow.
when my mother wouldn't get out of bed in the morning, akio was the one to get me out the door.
come on, he said, *let's go!*
and i followed him out the front door and into the woods.

† † †

do you think i should bother making my bed?
i pluck the seashell from under the pillow so i won't forget it. it's a weird shell—actually, it's a rock—but we call it a shell because my mother plucked it from the sea and gave it to me . . . and because it used to fit perfectly in my hand and over my ear like a shell. i used it like a phone.

whoops—*shōnen #4*—caught between the edge of the mattress and the wall. might as well crawl under the covers and hunt down all six of them.

it's probably stupid to sleep with my books, especially when they're already falling apart and you can't buy them anywhere. basically, they deserve a shrine—but i add them in a neat little stack to the pile in the center of the room, and i can't help myself, i grab the top book and flip it open to the first page:

is it dangerous to look too deeply?
on a street corner in the decayed city, there was a human dressed in black rags who had forgotten she once was a goddess in the crystal realm. she was half hidden behind her bat wing of a parasol, and at first glance, she seemed as delicate as a shadow, easily erased in the too-bright sun. . . .

i've been tricked by books all my life—

they fall into your hands at the exact right moment and say just what you need to hear—more like a friend than a book—until the moment you finish. as soon as you close the cover, the book goes back to being just words, just a memory of someone else's story—leaving you lonelier than you were before.

the reason i keep the shōnen books close is that they have never stopped being my friends, and you never know when you might have to reach for one.

sometimes i'll even have conversations with the books at night—i developed this method when i first came here.

† † †

we have to shut off the lights in the bedrooms after ten p.m.—but you can sneak read if you hang out of your bed and catch the fire escape light falling through the window.

first i pick a book—they all have different personalities—then i ask it a question, something like: *when will it happen?*

then i open to a random page, and whatever box my finger lands on, there's my answer. just a few marks on the page, a simple drawing—but everything inside that box is richly encoded with so many possible meanings.

i've been doing it for so many years that i don't really think about it. i don't stop and think how psychotic or abnormal it might be, because it feels completely right to me. sometimes i even talk to just one of the characters in the book, in my mind, opening and shutting and pointing and asking them things and imagining that they are asking me things too, like a real conversation.

† † †

so i get into a pretty good rhythm, going through all my drawers, tackling the stuff in the closet—but i could concentrate better if my brother wasn't knocking.

first of all, he isn't knocking on my door. he's knocking on the wall that divides our rooms. he also doesn't stop at two, four, five knocks. he keeps going. and while he knocks, he says, *knock, miya, miya, knock. knock, knock, me knock, miya, me knock, miya!*

he waits.

a muffled giggle.

our nightly routine, and he always starts up when i'm completely immersed in something. this could go on forever, and it will—until i answer.

but i don't have to give in right away.

† † †

stuff sorted—almost.
suitcase—i'll grab it in a sec.
what i really need is to get in touch with matsu.
so i go to see if she's online—

but when i get to her space, i have that sense of accidentally walking into the wrong house—

her ponderous gothic music, with the church organ of doom: gone.
the whole gothic lolita atmosphere: gone.
instead: girlish, tinkly music, little plum blossoms drifting gently across the page, a cupcake-colored theme.

she's still got that one picture of herself, but instead of

dominating her whole site, it's smaller, tucked into a corner. in the photograph, she's got that typical cocky matsu look in her eyes, chin held up, daring you to insult her. she's in victorian maiden-meets-kyoto-vampire—a strict, loli couture look—all black roses and ophelia crepe and embroidered corsets and gossamer delicacy. a thousand-dollar outfit, gorgeous black-and-white photograph.

one of the biggest lolita stores—lord sparrow—did a fashion shoot using street kids. no one got paid, but they each got this one moment of glory, posing on the famous omotesandō bridge, in harajuku—the same place where matsu and i spent the whole amazing day together, so long ago.

they didn't let her keep the clothes, but you can almost see the dark magic of the garments working on her—knotting her into a twisted enchantment that would set up a craving for more beautiful clothes, at any cost.

it's so obvious to me in that picture that she's struggling to look the loli part—elegant, regal, feminine—but inside she is more like a wild pirate, rough and vital, the type who would rather be in a boxing match or doing handstands.

but this war between her two sides—the real matsu and the gothic lolita matsu—is what really makes the picture so beautiful to me.

she was fifteen at the time, it was right after she ran away from here, and she had us both convinced that she was starting a glamorous new life there. she had a fantasy that they were going to choose her and turn her into a real model.

that picture's been on her site forever, and i don't blame her for not replacing it.

she used to have one of the best collections of loli links and videos—all wiped out—and now she has these creepy new glittery things, half a dozen corny phrases, things an innocent japanese schoolgirl would write:
may the tenderness of the sun's rays shine on everyone today.
happiness is yours if you try and smile.

each phrase is a link, so i click on one and gasp, because it leads me to a photograph of her in a very trashy pose—along with an invitation: *to see more . . .*

† † †

another round of knocks.
jesus, okay, i say to the wall. *who's there?*
hysterical throaty laughter.
you're so not cute, i tell him.
i should not encourage him. but there's no way to stop him.
soon he'll be asking for the book.

† † †

i didn't quite believe matsu when she told me about the "love hotels";
she bragged to me about it, not long after she ran away to tokyo. all the girls who wanted high-end designer clothes were picking up extra money that way—it was nothing, she told me, the guys she saw were just like "uncles."

all you had to do was let them buy you a drink, get a little tipsy—
some of those places even had hot tubs with bubbles!

or a tv so big, it took up the entire wall.
she watched cartoons the whole night, supposedly.
she said you could get through anything by concentrating on the amazing clothes you were going to get with all the money.

i begged her not to tell me any more details.

† † †

my brother's kicking the wall, and he's switched to his second mantra:
MIYATHEBOOK MIYATHEBOOK MIYATHEBOOK.

he wants book number six; so do i. if i have to pick a favorite, this is probably it, because it's the most romantic in the series. it's the only one my brother wants to hear, for some reason, and you'd think i would be sick of it by now, but i'm already on the floor thumbing through it, looking for the part i'll read to him tonight.

i read just a page or two, then, *bam*—i'm back in the story, heart beating as fast as if i had jumped off a mountain and swung into the center of the action.

i love this scene.

shōnen's surrounded by disciples of all ages, concentrating on transmitting the knowledge of the rainbow warrior. i can see him so clearly—deep eyes, a beautiful mouth—*a smile tinged with loss.*
they are outside, *in a meadow ringed by pines, the sun turning the fallen pine needles into a perfume.*
he knows that a handful of his students are plotting to overthrow him—but he seems oblivious to the girls who are crushing all over him.
or maybe he knows.
probably he knows.
the whole point is that he's one of the most highly aware beings in the universe, so *obviously* he knows.
he's just being loyal to 009.

for ten millenniums, they ruled the crystal realm together—until she fell, in one terrible instant, into the depths of shadowland, answering the cries of a lost child.

shōnen lives for the moments they can share together—but that doesn't stop the cutest girls from falling at his feet and trying to find new ways to tempt him.

i love the moments when he manifests in the human realm and the two lovers are briefly reunited—*in a primordial forest, in the early dawn, exactly at the apex of the equinox . . . holding each other for mere seconds, their embrace as delicate as it was torturous, gothiclolita009 was forced to ride the edge between ecstasy and certain loss—*

then *clump, clump, clump*—and my door flies open.

my brother is in my room, hugging his board to his chest, clutching the filthy string of the vacuum cleaner motor that he drags around like a pet.

miya—the book. the tone of a man trying to be patient, even though the report was due days ago.
not now, i tell him.
miyathebookmiyathebook! rising alarm, helpless desperation, the usual—so i start to pick him up to carry him over to the bed—

and he goes rigid.
fine! i hand it over.

i don't like giving up my book, but this happens sometimes. it's either that or pull out every trick i know to convince him to stay in my room and hear it . . . and then, of course, he'll want to hear the same passage again and again—anyway, he'll be back soon, demanding i read it.
i give him two minutes.

† † †

how will i deal with him? an image of the future lurches into my vision—
some cheap rented room in some unknown city, or maybe even an abandoned building? how will i deal with him if we don't have separate rooms and there is no adult to back me up? what will i do if he starts screaming, even tonight on the last train out—or if we have to hide? and where are we going, anyway?

† † †

there's a dull pain behind my eyes and i snap off my light, throwing the room into eerie shadows.

† † †

at my desk.
mouth dry, heart in my throat,
staring into the screen until i see spots.
how can i lay it all out to you if i can't even write a first sentence? how about:
i want to talk to you so bad. desperate!
or: *i'm going to give up on you.* a lie.
dark things flit through me.
don't you care that i exist?
delete that.
it's been three years—
can't you break your silence?
can't you hear me scream?
too intense, even if it's real.
there's something i want to tell you.

CHELSEA:

i was addicted to watching tokyo videos on youtube and i kept imagining i could spot you in the middle of the harajuku street scene.

the lonely man episode 93

Rate: ★★★★★ 1,304 ratings **Views:** 939,921

Share | Favorite | Playlists | Flag

Mydamnspace Girlbloggers Makeaworld (more share options)

Commentary | **Statistics & Data**

Video Responses: **0** Text Comments: **1,147**

▶ **Video Responses** (0) **Sign in to post a Video Response**

MIYA:
all i knew is you lived in hollywood
and were into gothic lolita.

Chelsea

PART FIVE. LOS ANGELES.

1.

i keep seeing you.

i'm at the red light, breathing in pure diesel, cars whizzing by. school's just across the street.

when i see you, there's a certain spot—just in front of my vision, slightly to the left—but it's not your face.
it's not even an image. it's just you.
maybe you're not telling me everything, but you have shown more than you know. i would recognize you—not just from the pictures you posted, but with my eyes closed, somehow.
i would know your essence.

we have such an intense connection—but what use is it? it's like what happened with memphis, when i was in elementary school.

when i was at school and memphis was little, there were random moments he'd pop into my mind. the vision would have such force that i would make a note of the time—and when i got home, mom would give me the report: *2:15!*—and that would be the time he went off. sometimes even screaming my name.

so that's how it is when i see you: when you pop up the strongest, i worry about you. but there's nothing i can do about it. it's not a good, warm feeling, like it used to be. it's a twisted feeling like i had about memphis, when i sensed he was in trouble and i couldn't help. like what can i do for you, if you're not here with me?

what total b.s.

there are things i can do that would instantly change your life.

as i was reminded only yesterday by mom.
i hate her for putting me in this position—and i hate myself for not jumping to help you. but she never should have gotten involved.
have to admit i've been avoiding her calls since she got on

the plane for japan, but we finally connected yesterday. replay of our phone convo:
she: trying to sound neutral, but completely trying to get me to agree to the adoption.
me: adamant—she can do what she wants. but i'm not in.
she: on edge of tears.
me: telling her to quit the friggin' guilt trip and just do whatever she wants.
she: insisting that the two of us are still a family and she respects me too much to make a decision without me.
me: okay then, mom.
she: launching right back in with arguments about our empty house, her hefty retirement funds, the moral imperative—basically, why it should happen according to her EZ 1-2-3, time-to-save-the-world plan.

when she talks to me like that, it's like she has forgotten the holiness of the situation and reduced it to something logical.

painful equation: two new kids will never be equal to my one brother and her one son. even when one of those kids is you.

have you forgotten everything that's sacred? shōnen moved

closer to 009, even as she avoided his eyes. *have you forgotten that the only way to stop the world is to exist between the molecules of all the choices and connect with that one atom of truth?*
um, maybe? said 009.
come on, he said. *you can do better than that. pay attention, that's all you need to do.*

and i have been paying attention.

by keeping detached from everything that is false and transitory. by holding everything at a distance except for that one atom of truth—that my brother lives. but today i must think of you as well.
i don't know how i came to hold your fate.

† † †

i feel like i am the only person in the universe fighting to keep a space open so my brother can return.

how many days have i started out feeling strong, feeling like a human with dignity instead of a little gopher, then walk straight into the trap—instantly poisoned by the atmosphere of school, forgetting everything i thought i knew?

it's been three years since he disappeared, and the outside world is what weakens me, what makes me lose hope with its false intrusions.

i feel you calling to me and i feel my mother. this decision is squeezing my skull. it would be so easy to lose myself in the fake world of school, to let it suck me in and make me dizzy enough to forget what's real. all i can do is pray for wisdom and strength.

i make this vow to not lose it, to hold on to the reality that i choose, the one i own. i tune my molecules to that reality and pledge to stay in pitch with it even as i am on the verge of entering the world of chaos and illusion, where there is a different kind of singing, and i will not sing their songs or hear their words as long as i keep this reality intact.

my brother, you, the mountain—this is all i want to know today, and let nothing else touch me.

i will not give up what matters the moment i get to school.

PART SIX. JAPAN.

1.

there are things i want to tell you—
but for now i have to keep in motion.
i sneak past my brother—on his bed, pretending to read out loud to himself—and i'm in matsu's old room.
there's nothing left of her here.

the room smells clean, powdery—small crib in the corner, soft baby things folded on the bed, and casually tossed at the foot of the bed, that sweater the american's always wearing.

it's warm, woven in gossamer yarn, rich colors. i snug it around myself for a second—i knew it would feel so cozy and weightless—then toss it just as casually back onto her bed.

her bag is completely open on the chair.
big roll of cash on top.
and: her cell phone, a really nice one.

americans are so careless.
and also: a skinny silver tube of lipstick, which i pluck right out like it's a sweet rose in an endless garden, and i lean into matsu's old mirror and slick it onto my mouth.
toss it back in the american's bag.
i would like something darker and shinier and more sheer.
and i would like to take her phone, because i really want to call matsu and i don't want to use the phone downstairs.
i grab an empty suitcase from matsu's old closet, carrying it instead of wheeling it, passing soundlessly back to my room.

† † †

so what do you think of these boots, take them or leave them?
the truth is, my clothes are crap.
everything i own is part of a plan.
an item to remind me of what i could do, if that item would just multiply itself into a whole outfit.

these rainbow tights. this black veil i found in the leaves that time with matsu. this skirt she gave me—i've never even worn it. too perfect.

matsu was so pissed at me. she gave me the skirt out of pity, but more than anything, she was pissed. i remember the way she threw it at me. her face was twisted with emotion.

she was so mad at me for not buying clothes.
the funny thing is that she was right—i could have spent it all with her that day, instead of tagging along, store after store, pretending i didn't see anything i liked. the idea was to save for a good doctor for my brother instead of the clinic they take him to at the hospital. i felt almost noble at the time, but in reality, there is nothing worse than sacrificing yourself for a worthless idea.

worthless because i probably had enough for half a doctor's visit—as if i could even find a doctor and get my brother there. and worthless because my brother's perfect the way he is.

so i could have gotten clothes. at the same time, there wasn't anything i really wanted.

2.

we'd woken up too early—i'd gotten drunk for the first (and only) time with matsu and her friends and gone to see fireworks. we were in harajuku for less than an hour when i started to go on overload. elvis boys on skateboards. thizzled-out rubber buggi dancers facing off with the stylized para para girls.

it was the first time away from the home—and from my brother, since he was born. but even the women who ran the home practically forced me to take two days away, to stay with my so-called relative. matsu was brilliant at those sorts of things. but just being out of my own little town was enough to make me feel my head was no longer attached to my body. add to that the trouble i'd gotten into the night before . . . and everything on the bridge and the plaza made me feel like i was walking on a tilting raft in the middle of a psychedelic sea.

we crossed yoyogi park, into the expensive section of mostly restaurants and designer boutiques.

tourists were lined up to get into a victorian maiden café. my heart leaped when i saw the four posh lolis, seated at tiny white tables, beneath a pink and white canopy, sipping tea.

at first glance, these girls were my ideal: waif eyes, starving eyes. short skirts. all of them with delicate lace undergarments and weblike, weightless stockings. i checked out their complicated victorian lace-up boots—they belonged in shoe museums.

they seemed so perfect—until matsu started picking them apart, rattling off the designers of their pieces, along with the prices: $600 for that one's moi-même-moitié dress, $200 for that pair of mile-high innocent aristocrat shoes etched with the cutest pink squirrels. . . .

i felt a guilty, dissatisfied excess, like i'd ripped through twenty expensive presents and not found
the one small, huggable doll i craved.

i stayed quiet.

we walked around for hours, staring, getting stared at, eating stuff, dancing by the stage.

outside i saw another one of *them:* she was cradling an eyeless doll, kneeling in the shadows of a massive tree. i'd seen these scary lolitas once before—when i came here with my mother.

the crowd was moving away without casting her a glance, but i moved closer. i got close enough to touch her if i wanted to. she stayed frozen, her eyes without light, like those of a severely traumatized child who has completely retreated to another world.

a black veil climbed over her face like crumbly spiderwebs, her legs were black lace, her boots were also black. i got closer, eager to stand next to her—but also shy. she looked straight at me then, and i saw a greenish light swimming in her dark eyes. i'll never forget the way she passed those eyes over me and the way she smiled—a dignified and private smile.

after hours of being visually bombarded by new and expensive and bright clothes, this girl's clothes seemed even more beautiful to me because they were old and worn, looking like they were all she ever put on. her clothes clung darkly to her body; you couldn't buy the dirt on her peeled leather boots or the disintegrating dust of her used stockings. i could see her sleeping in them or sleeping nude, preferring to have nothing else touch her skin.

where would she live? i wanted to follow her home. what would her apartment be like—lonely and small as a closet? certainly she didn't have a mother.

i began to realize what she meant to me. no matter that my face was scrubbed clean and i wore jeans and a t-shirt and my hair was pulled back in a careless ponytail. when i saw this girl, it was like looking in a mirror.

† † †

back at matsu's apartment, when she was done being psychotic, she gave me some of her old things. she used a slick bag from the hottest boutique—monkey showers—and filled it to the top, wrapping her barely used clothes in purple tissue.

it was autumn then, gray and about to rain. i remember how it was, walking back to the train home. i tried to feel happy and be grateful for the weight of all the new stuff in my bag. crossing the park, and there—half concealed in a pile of rotted leaves—i found the missing piece: a delicate veil, shredded, worn, something a vampire would hide behind when the moon was too bright for her eyes. i stuck it in the black and purple monkey showers bag, on top of all the tissue-wrapped goodies, and i'm trying it on now, peering at myself through the crumbles.

i wish i had some of that stuff now, but i was so depressed when i got home, i shoved all of it in the trash—except for the skirt, i couldn't get rid of this skirt. now i slip it on and smooth it over my hips in the mirror. i'm basically the same size i was when i was thirteen. it was way too small for matsu's curves. i secretly think of this as the lolichan16 skirt, because i imagine it's so elegant i could wear it to that cosplay café on melrose. knee-length, bell-shape, double-frilled around the hem, cut beautifully from the densest dark fabric.

i flash on that ancient fairy tale about a girl falling in love with a pair of red shoes when she should have been thinking about her family. i step out of the skirt and toss it in the suitcase before i can change my mind.

† † †

it's stupid to be thinking about clothes at a time like this, but maybe not. maybe this is when your life flashes before your eyes, and all you see is a bunch of crap clothes. but at least i still have most of my money. about $200—that will really get us far.

† † †

i start throwing things in the suitcase, and my heart speeds up like an insane drum: *we're really doing this.*

3.

anyone would think i was crazy if they knew that i talked to you all the time.
not out loud.
but, still, it's crazy to talk to a spirit twin,
even in your mind.
probably even more insane that i think you're lolichan16.

i don't know when it started getting swirled together
in my mind—
not true. i know exactly when.

it started with this computer.
i know—hideous, slow, giant—
but it was thrilling and perfect when they surprised me with it on my eleventh birthday.
i was on girlbloggers before breakfast and wrote my first blog—something like: *HI, what's ^??? :)*
heart pounding as i posted it.
waiting.
for what?
for my first reader.

there was no mad rush.
so i started looking for blogs to read.

i cruised around worlds where dolls lived and cartoons were real.

j-rock girls, gladiator elves, punky bo-peeps, and cowboy godzillas—but mostly, all types of loli girls. everything i saw turned into paper dolls in my head; i spent the night between dream and waking, mixing and matching frothy skirts and gothic purses, adding ribbons and roses, raising and lowering the heels of boots, fashioning an eternity of outfits in my mind.

i fixed up my profile the next day, adding some tags. *gothic lolita*, of course, even though i barely knew what they were.

i hesitated over *cosplay*. while i was cruising around i caught a heated debate on an american lolita thread—some of the lolis despised the cosplay kids. cosplay kids mostly dressed like their favorite manga and game characters and the snotty lolitas seemed miles above that. but i liked the look of the cosplay kids so i left it as a tag.

i have to admit, you found me first.

my heart was slamming when i saw your little icon flashing on my page. so i went to your page and—instant recognition! the mist-shrouded trees and forlorn music, everything done with such stark beauty—it spoke to me.

both of us were liked scared little chickens, blocking all comments. and neither of us requested to be each other's girlbloggers friend. but i would catch you on my page almost every day. it became a game of hide-and-seek. i'd read you, you'd read me, both of us barred from commenting.

i didn't know much about you.
your name: lolichan16.
your shortest hotlist in the universe:
gothic lolita, cosplay, and the name of some manga i'd never seen.
but you lived in hollywood, and that said it all.

† † †

i've imagined you in a mansion, if you want to know the truth. a pink and gold mansion surrounded by palm trees, in hollywood, with a turquoise pool. or sometimes a luxury high-rise, every room white, and yours with a canopy bed and a room-size mirrored closet and a perfect little balcony. and you'd sit there in the sunshine, surrounded by pots of jasmine and roses, gazing down at your sparkling turquoise pool.

i looked up cosplay in hollywood, and i found lolipopland on melrose—*the one-stop loli café and boutique*—where all the posh lolitas and sweet lolitas and trendy new cutting-edge surf lolitas and victim lolitas and punk lolitas hung out having tea parties and eating little cakes and pouring tea for one another at frilly tables in the back looking out onto the pond with real swans gliding past. i saw it all on youtube, and it reminded me of the café i glimpsed in harajuku, that day with matsu. but the hollywood café seemed even more like it was peeled out of a gorgeous storybook. i replayed the videos again and again, wishing i could climb into the action. i imagined i could see you there, strolling about. sometimes you were all in white, sometimes in an alice-in-wonderland-meets-the-pirates look—all red and black and dashing—and sometimes classic lolita, the most elegant girl in the group. your look changed with my mood.

remember that time you put the photo of the inside of your fridge in there? you would put pictures up mostly without any captions, and i would just guess who everyone was. i'd been reading you for ages, hoping for a picture of one human—and then one day, there it was: you posted a photograph of a beautiful little boy—around four or five, with long hair and a charming smile, with cheeks you just want to kiss—and you wrote: *i could never say . . . or try to explain . . . how much this kid means to me.*
i guessed he was your brother, and i was a little jealous—to have someone you could love so much, and someone so adorable! back then, i was an only child. . . .

one thing i was crazy to know was: where could i get that manga on your hotlist? i spent hours looking it up—i tried a million different spellings. not one mention anywhere. when i was older, i even asked for it in a bookstore, and it was as if it existed only in your mind.

but we could never ask each other anything,
we never broke our silence.
there would be hints—
you would put up an angry kitty pic and say *mood: morbid*—
and i would know that you weren't seriously desolate. but
that time you posted a photograph of some blurry leaves . . .
and the next day—an elephant chained to a post. *mood: choked.*
drastic measures were needed.
so i posted that photo of mt. fuji—and now
it's confession time.
yes, i see it every day of my life. i mean EVERY DAY OF MY LIFE. even when you're in tokyo, you can see it.
but i never climbed it.
it seemed more inspiring to say *i went here today*
than *i'm too lazy to imagine going near this thing.*
did it even cheer you up?

† † †

neither of us missed more than a few days, ever.
for two years.
obviously, the computer is too big to bring.

4.

i was helping my father clean out my grandmother's attic after she died. it was so narrow, you had to crawl. there was one last box just beyond my fingertips, barely bigger than a shoe box.

i could see it, but every time i tried to grab it, i pushed it a bit farther away. something in me just had to get my hands on the box.

but i finally gave up and left it and forgot all about it for a few weeks, until they sold the house and one rainy day i was standing in my doorway, watching the new people move in and suddenly i splashed out into the rain and shoved past the new people, ran up her stairs, and reached in—and somehow got my fingernails around the edges and pulled it out—and that's how i found the shōnen series when i was thirteen.

six complete issues, packed into a plain box, slightly used but in perfect condition—except the last page of the last book was ripped out.

the box had a postmark from hollywood, and it had been mailed in care of my grandma's house, only a few weeks earlier. she must have gotten it and stashed it in the attic right before she died.

my grandma had been a bizarre and enigmatic woman, and this was just one more layer to her mystery.

† † †

the name of the manga jumped out at me—*shōnen rainbow warrior*—familiar, like something i'd seen every day. so at first i thought, *right, i've been hearing about this one for years.*

i perched on the attic steps, skimming the inside cover:

gothiclolita009, *once the beloved ruler of the crystal realm, is now trapped in the material world known as shadowland, where the law of the world is chaos and greed.*

shōnen *has a daring new plan to send rainbow warriors into the human realm to lift the massive suffering—but if he makes one false move, he will destroy the covenant of ultimate truth . . . and lose 009 forever.*

will shōnen's rescue mission succeed*—or will it fail, causing eternal darkness to reign?*

it all hinges on 009*—she MUST remember her true identity and find her way back through the portal.*

and then my test for any new manga: opening to a random page—

one by one, the bravest warriors began to enter the material realm as babies, enraged and screaming, with zero tolerance for the normal human ways, their true nature concealed behind the mask of wrathful deities. . . .

everything i wanted in a manga—romance, drama, fantasy, horror—and grandma was always talking about wrathful deities. i came back to myself with a start.
my grandmother and mother were gone,
and our house was wrapped in grief.
it felt wrong to be drawn in by a book again, and yet something about this book tugged at me.

it had stopped raining, and the smell of dirt and flowers

was clinging to the damp air coming in through the attic window. the truth slipped into my mind as gently as the warmth of the day: the only place i had ever heard of the shōnen series was on your girlbloggers space.

holding the proof of its existence made you suddenly more real.
i ran to my blog—and broke our tradition by writing directly to you.

lolichan16, i found the shōnen series!

i posted without even thinking, the dark clouds scattered for another moment—
all i knew was it was time for us to finally connect.

then i went to your blog—

but for the first time in years, there was nothing.

and the next day—nothing.

it's been three years.

where did you go, lolichan16? did i scare you off?

† † †

when you disappeared, the truth settled into me.
the books came not long after you stopped posting. and they weren't just any books . . . i knew the day that i got them that you were not just some girl on a blog.

she was born immediately to someone else.

i've always felt our connection, like an invisible cord that feeds us both. it comforts me to imagine that you're in the world. sometimes i wonder if we're living a parallel existence. whenever you see those stories about twins who were separated at birth, it's like their wiring is still attached. they end up marrying the same kind of guy, having the same brand of car . . . it happens all the time! we weren't those kinds of twins, obviously. but if you're out there and you can hear me, i wish you'd give me a sign.

† † †

i can hear them downstairs, tv going, pots clattering in the kitchen. soon the younger ones will be heading up for their baths. maybe i'll even wait until everyone's asleep.

i've got a few more things to pack, but it's going to happen tonight. i'm going to grab my brother's hand, we're going to walk through that door. there's no other choice but out.

are you with me?

where r u?

Chelsea

PART SEVEN. LOS ANGELES.

1.

i've made it to the edge of school
and i want to turn right around.
all i have to do is get within earshot of a school, any school, and my father's ancient advice smacks me over the head: *the first thing to do is get your game face on.*

the emerson high parking lot is vast, the air charged with tension and reefer, snatches of reggaeton and hip-hop pumping from the cars. the whole place feels more like a party than the first morning of school. i want to be home, back in my bed—the room dark, air conditioner on, under the covers, watching cartoons.

i miss memphis. i miss him so strong, it feels like the only thing moving through my veins.
i can't imagine walking into a classroom or opening a book—

we'll be together again.

i'm going to let that thought be the one cold, sharp thing.
i won't let it vanish, no matter what happens at school.

he's not gone.

if i can focus on that, i will pull him back to me.

if i let go of it, he will be gone.

i won't forget what is real.

when the warning bell shrills, i let it pull me in deeper.

† † †

my father's voice kicks in.

where's your game face, kid? my father gave me a quick, tight smile. we were parked in front of the elementary school, first day of first grade, me in the backseat, my parents acting like they were sending me into a war zone.

my father's voice always kicks in on the first day of school. how many years has it been—nine, ten? i'll probably hear him on the first day of college, saying the same thing.

come on, brian, my mother said. *chels doesn't even know what* game face *means.*

the morning was bursting with energy—parents singing out good-byes, kids pouring into the school—it gave me a twist of nerves, but it was a good twist. i had new clothes and a new lunch box and i didn't need a game face.

my father drummed his fingers on the steering wheel. *look at them, wearing their masks.* he squinted out at the kids like they were miniature suicide bombers. *you've got to study them, chels, study and learn.* a pulse ticked on the side of his neck, and it felt like any second he might squeal away from the curb before i could even go inside.

mom put her hand over his—*brian . . .*
sorry, kid. he shot me a sheepish glance in the rearview mirror. *i'm a lunatic.*
we all kind of relaxed a little, but then he leaned over like

a chess player and, with one twist of the mirror, forced me to look into my own shocked eyes. that's *what i'm talking about, dude. you can't walk around all exposed and defenseless like that. all la-la-la and bullcrap. you're like a perfect freaking target. you need your mask and you need a game face. just say it:* game face.
but, dad.

my mother made another little shushing, scolding sound. *just go and fit in with everyone,* she told me. *think of others and don't focus so much on yourself. you'll be happier that way.*

2.

i'm weaving through the lot, head down; kids hooking up, mini-reunions all around: *DUDE, how the EFF ARE you?* they're finding their own, and i'm invisible. i'm moving, but inside i'm a stalled machine. everything's just out of my reach, every trick i used to know.

another heart-stopping surge of music, and i catch a few girls throwing out quick and complicated dance moves; they're tightening and releasing their backs like animals i'm not related to.

† † †

i once knew how to move, i once was popular, and the thought comes to me with a sickening jolt, like remembering that you once punched someone in the face or made a baby cry.

† † †

the second bell slices through me, sparking off this fear of being lost—and i'm not even inside the school yet. i'm mentally pawing at the air, trying for something tangible:

room numbers, teachers' names—nothing.

i unzip my backpack for my schedule, and i flash on something—a dim, thousand-year-old memory: i shoved my schedule in my dang hello kitty purse. only i don't have my little hello kitty purse—in fact, my backpack is empty except for a crumpled gum wrapper and a pair of sunglasses. grabbed the wrong backpack. panic rolls into my gut, thick and slow, like it's going to be there for a while. and how did i get inside this limp black dress—did i just grab it off the floor this morning? i feel like an amnesia victim just waking up. *game face, game face.*

† † †

my father would have killed me for being such a mess. he was a decorated marine during the gulf war, and he was just as disciplined when he moved to l.a. afterward and became a maritime patroller. he was prepared when he went into enemy territory, and he was prepared when he met the waves.

my mother took a different approach—she wasn't fierce, but she wasn't a pushover. i got her dark hair, my father's green eyes. when things were good, i lived with a foot in each of their worlds, balanced in the middle of the galaxy.

that first morning of first grade, i kissed my mom; and she looked at me and she whispered, *i'll miss you.*

and then i really saw the quality that made her different: it was in her eyes and it shimmered around her face—a loneliness so deep that i felt some of it seeping into me as i pulled away from her hug.

just as i reached the school, my father called me back with a piercing whistle. my face burned. no one else was being whistled back to their car. i had a fleeting thought of ignoring him—but he'd know.
game face, he whispered, like a hypnotist. *if you can't actually do it, just say the words:* game face. *think of it as your magic mantra, kid.*

i said the words then and i'm saying them now, but the words don't keep you safe. there's only one thing that can make you lock in like a puzzle piece: your people—and i finally spot them, just at the edge of the lot.

3.

dylan—leaning up against his black jetta, talking smack with some guys; and mariah—wearing something tight and black and pink.
she's bending over to fix her shoe or some other excuse to flash her fuchsia low-cut boy shorts (i have a pair just like that somewhere, unless maybe it *is* mine).

i'm half grinning—i could just run up and snap the waistband and say, *hey, bitch, nice undies*—and destiny's there too, dressed in semi-cosplay, still in her bunni ears. but something holds me back.

all of them too caught up to notice me, but it's such a relief to see them—even with mariah cuddling up close to dylan, kind of getting right up under his arm. she's always so physical, even with girls—but it tugs at something inside me, an old, dull pain. why does she always have to be so flirty with *him*—and this time he's giving it back, pulling her in close and tight—are they kissing? i move away fast, plunging back into the crowds.

it makes sense dylan and mariah are together. of course they'd end up like that.

they're nothing to me.

they haven't been anything for three years.

a lapse, thinking they were my people. thinking i'd run over. stupid impulse.

i head up the walkway—a raised ramp with low walls on the sides, the only way into the school. numb. blank. no reason to get worked up over ancient, stupid trivia.

so why do i squeeze between two jocks, crane my neck, scan the crowd, and feel way more than i should when i spot my ex-pals all over again?

they're tiny as dolls, evil dolls.

mariah's swiveling her little head, and then i get it, she's looking for me, of course—it's like she can't really taste her victory until she sees my pain. we're way too far apart to be locking enemy eyes, but i know she's found me. she's holding on to dylan but looking at me—her face just a tiny cream-colored blur, but i can easily picture her smug expression: chin raised, mouth compressed, eyes glittering. i look away and all i see is a mess of scenes stitched together, all of them starring mariah.

4.

um, this is our spot? some skinny six-year-old with low-cut jeans and pink suspenders, standing over me in the middle row of the first-grade classroom. she said it like a question, but there was no doubt. she was just some bossy girl who ended up moving away a year or so later.

backing her up: another girl in identical jeans, this one chubbier, with clenched fists and a pinched mouth—mariah.

sorry, i mumbled, gathering my stuff, already scanning the room for another open desk.

oh. em. gee, the first girl said to my back. *did you see what she was wearing?*

yeah, said mariah. *puke.*

i whispered their intonations to myself, not to mimic them, but because it was fascinating to me the way they said each word so clearly and dramatically, like they were up onstage giving a play.

did you see what she was ***WEAR-ING****?*

puke.

word got out that i had a problem with my brain. that i was one of those kids who repeated things.

you're special ed, some kid told me. *and they stuck you in with us.*

i ran home to the *rainbow warrior* books my mother had given me; she was still using them to teach me japanese. i knew quite a bit of hirigana, the simple characters kids first learn in school—and i was starting to learn kanji. at first i was overwhelmed—but my desire to know the story kept pulling me on.

many times i didn't understand the words, even when mom translated them into english, but when i sat on my bed after school and read a sentence again and again, the meaning would sink into me, and later i would almost forget who had experienced it first—me or the character.

009 had passed through an invisible portal—and the rules on the other side were harsh and foreign; she did not know how to make herself fit in. . . .

5.

we call the walkway the *walk of shame.*
it has raised ledges on both sides, and every clique has its spot, and you're either one of the cool people on the ledges or you're one of the nothing people or freaks who have to crawl by.

it's like a reverse red carpet, and better not stare at the gang people or they'll jump off the wall and be on your throat. it's always been about which side of the line you're on, and i've been on both. but for the longest time, the lines were invisible to me. i didn't get where they were, what you had to do to cross over, or even why they existed.

† † †

it's three minutes before they lock the front doors, and the walkway's suddenly one big traffic jam. no one's shoving yet, but i catch two uniformed guards in the sunshine, drinking out of starbucks cups, ready. having the guards around makes everyone a little less reckless.

i'm behind this girl, and i can't even remember her name—she's wearing those thick, cheap fishnets and ill-made mary jane boots, fresh out of the hollywood mall's nastiest chain store—mariah'd be right down my throat for even talking to the girl, i can already hear the classic mariah hiss: *wannabe.*

when i was close with mariah, i was actually excited that there were people who would *wannabe* like us.

mariah took me in at the beginning of junior high, acting like we'd never had a problem before. i was her makeover-of-the-year project—she was going to turn me from do-it-yourself goth to an elegant gothic lolita, the darkest one of their clique. we would all hang out at lolipopland on melrose, dressed in our costumes, pouring each other tea.
i was their token asian. well, half-asian.

they all knew how to call each other *bitch.*
i used to practice it at home. *hi, bitch! what's up, bitch?*
hey, bitch.
i loved the way they effortlessly tossed things out: *he was kickin' it with her.*

they did it raw dog. a language i could hear but couldn't own.

i didn't realize it takes so much shared time to become part of a tribe; i felt like i was supposed to know all the secrets at once, as if their complex friendships could be reduced to something logical, like math problems, and put in a handbook and that book was just out of my reach.
but i hung out with them, and their knowledge seeped into me. i got my own mask—and my mother was the first to complain about the fit:

why do you have that look on your face, what's that new weird laugh, why are you acting like that?

but it felt good to talk like others, to walk their walk.
by seventh grade, i was part of the tribe.

† † †

i want to give that mall girl a giant lesson in protocol.
i used to be a freak like you, i could tell her. *and the first thing you have to do is stop being so obvious.*

the girl is all over the place—big grin on her face, openly
gawking at all the fringe looks and gang bling.

of course i'm checking out the emerson elite, everyone is—
there's this one girl on the ledge who has two-inch blue hair
and a matching blue dog paw tattoo on her neck.
and no eyebrows, chewed-up nails, and a tight, small mouth.
yes, my cowardly heart thumps. *yes, she's scary.*

6.

what chew lookin' at with yur stank ho face? says the dog paw girl.
ice runs through me, only she's not talking to me, she's talking to—
the mall girl.

the mall girl's mouth is open a little, the way innocent girls always let their mouths go slack when they're caught off guard, and it definitely catches you off guard to be called a stank ho, but stank ho or not, can't this mall person close her mouth? *game face, bitch! where's your game face?*

ah, she's useless—and she's going to cave. she's going to back down and grovel before that dog paw girl.

the others are pressing in, mildly curious. i can hear the ticking of their little minds: would the incident bulge into an ugly scene, staining the walkway with someone's blood, making us all late? oh, god, please.

my cell rings. no one hears it but me—everyone else is

craning to hear the next piece of drama—

sorry, the mall girl mutters.

the blue paw leader looks down with hard slit eyes, considering. offers the most miserly of nods. you can hear the collective sigh of relief. or is it disappointment?

the mall girl moves on, with slightly bowed head. lesson learned. no more goony gaping. the mall girl moves on, but—

i can't.

i hate myself for shrinking back, looking the other way, doing nothing—even though it's in my mind to take action.

all at once, my brother's entire essence rushes at me in a crushing hug—
his orange sweater warm, holding the scent of his day—
dirt and pennies—green wood, chocolate milk—
everything that is specifically and only memphis, it's all crushed into me and gone as quick as it came, leaving me

feeling like a bomb went off
in my head.

i was supposed to remember. i'd promised myself to not get sucked into first-day school drama. and what did it take—two minutes for me to forget my brother and you your brother? i hate myself for being human.

† † †

when memphis was around, i was a superhero. i could always take the right action if i remembered that he was watching. not our father's way. and not our mother's.

there was a third way to live, the way memphis and i lived for a few years, and everything we learned came from *rainbow warrior*.
as soon as i understand one of shōnen's secret techniques for dealing with humans, i passed it on to my brother. and the first lesson was how to stop the world.

7.

the denizens of the crystal realm are free to appear in shadowland—but only as constantly changing and subtle illusions—minuscule rainbows, totemic gods at the seam between water and land, sometimes disguised as twig and rock. . . .

i was ten years old, and on book four of the shōnen series, when memphis was two. even though the books inspired all our games by then, i didn't quite look at the powers as something literal or possible for people like us—until the day we were in a specialist's office, and memphis was curled up on the floor in the only shaft of sun. he had one eye closed and the other squinting at the fistful of hair he held in his hand. he was making tiny, tiny motions of his head. he would not move from this position. when dad tried to pick him up onto the examining table, he shrieked and went right back into the spot in the sun.

. . . all nearly invisible to the human eye, evading detection by shifting form . . .

the doctor took my parents into an inner office to throw around some more of the long words that meant nothing and showed no kind of cure.
i curled up next to memphis, close enough to breathe in the faintly spring scent of his glossy, too-long black hair.
i grabbed a few strands of my own hair and squinted at them close to my face, exactly like memphis, holding them in the sun, to see what i could see.

. . . *only those gifted with special powers will know how to see them. and the first power is to stop the world.*

and there it was. the sun turned my hair into dozens of miniature prisms, with minute touches of electric color quivering on top of each strand—and when i moved my head in tiny shakes, the colored lights danced and twinkled, shifting to new shades.

this tiny, minuscule, subtle thing couldn't possibly be what he was transfixed by—but i knew it was. and there was no way i was going to bring the doctor and my parents in and convince them to see what my brother saw and had taught me to see.

i would never convince them of anything, because they didn't know how to stop the world.

† † †

in only a moment, i let myself forget.
i got sucked right back into the fake world;
all it took was mariah and dylan and a girl in a bad outfit.
time to exit this hell.
time to be alone with my thoughts and face the question of the day.

8.

edging back down the walk of shame, against the tide, dizzying to be the one dark fish swimming upstream, and yet unnoticed, sliding past face after blank face, it's almost a game now, seeing how many eyes i can meet without anyone looking back at me—whoops, dylan and mariah, hanging on each other, squeezing past me, close enough to make me wobble from his arm brushing up against mine, breathing in his clean, familiar scent—i try to catch his eyes, but he really doesn't see me. both of them look right through me and i keep going, but maybe i don't keep going, because maybe i don't even exist.

† † †

my cell is ringing again.
probably mom.
i just can't handle talking to her now.
but when it stops, i play back the message.
and even with the noise of the school crowd, i can hear it. i can hear japan. for just a second, i hear a woman in the background yelling to someone in japanese. i hear a bird.

a *japanese* bird. mom must have gone outside.

hi, babe, it's late, is the first thing she says. *almost midnight here. i don't want to pressure you, but it's time, it's really time.*
so much for the bird. caged bird? no bird at all? IS THERE SUCH A THING AS A FREAKING NIGHTBIRD?
japan. she's there.
i'm not.
my jealous heart is roaring so loudly that i have to play her message back again. *hey, chels, i guess you're just getting into school—i'm sorry i'm not there—but sweetie, you have to let me know what you've decided.*
have a beautiful day! love you so much!

i don't call her back.
there's only one person i want to talk to and that's you.

M&C

PART EIGHT.

1. Miya

are you on the other side?
because i feel you're so close tonight.
the only thing between us is words—neither of us dares to speak.
i try a few more beginnings—delete everything almost as quickly as i type it.
it's almost midnight and my brother never came back to annoy me. obviously sleeping.
should go pack some of his things. starting to feel like i can't really do this tonight.
help.
if only you could.
what do i want from you, anyway?
too much to ask from one human.
i feel like crashing my computer against the wall. it's been the thing that's tormented me for so long—

† † †

i fall back onto my bed and curl into a ball—i'm going to miss this room. tiniest room in the house, but every choice in the world seems to exist between my windows—ocean and forest above my bed, and by my desk, a view of the train station.

the trains streak in and out every hour, for tokyo, and of course i think of getting on one, at least twice a day.

it's not the room i'm going to miss—it's what's *out there.*

the outside world has always felt more like home to me than any house.

† † †

when i stand on my bed and look through the farthest corner of the window, i can make out the forest, a dark blur, and beyond the trees, i can see the tiny triangle of the ocean that seems so alive, i can nearly see sparks of moonlight on the waves.

there are hot surfer boys down there sometimes,

even this time of night.

i could be there in ten minutes if i ran.

but i don't care about hot surfer boys—
it's the forest.

† † †

i used to imagine you looking out your windows at your swimming pool. . . .

here, you'd move between my views, pacing like a tiger. you'd look out at the red station lights bleeding onto the river, and you would probably jump out the window and grab the next train out.

but i'm the one who's trying to escape. all these years and all these things i've kept from you. it feels like i have to clear away a tangled forest with my bare hands to get to some of it.

† † †

the thing about the forest—it was right outside my door.
i'd wake excited every morning because something was there in the woods, calling to me, and my mother couldn't keep me.

i'd thrown on jeans, a shirt—
where are you going? she'd say. *stop!*

i'd walk on the pounded-down path, then i'd run, i might fly, because *it was all there,* in the forest, waiting for me, one continual game that stretched out longer than time, like a story strip above your head.

i was there even when it rained, even in the dark. it was my corner of paradise—up until the day i came home and heard my mother yelling from behind our locked door: *they're coming, they're coming—*
my hand was shaking—i was already screaming out, *MOM!*
she was half on, half off the couch, crouched like an animal, a teakettle screeching in the kitchen.

and she was on the telephone with grandma, my hello kitty watch in her trembling hand, trying to time her own contractions. when she saw me, she dropped the phone, reaching her hand up to me.
my water broke, miya.

a new me climbed into my body to put a calming arm around

my mother, to set my mother up on the couch and put a cloth over her, which we soon both forgot about when she just had time to peel off her maternity sweatpants, spread her legs, and scream a baby into the world, both of their faces equally purple and with a huge dark handful of hair, and i did not want to touch either of them but here was this thing framed by her stretched *thing*, and my mother screaming like death, this ball of hair, the scrunched face and its bluishbrownsilvery eyes open, looking at *me*, how could it look at me when it wasn't even out, because it was alive, without being out, that's how, and i had to get it *out*, she was all stretched and screaming, *it's burning, it's burning, i'm being torn in two,* and then she held her breath and groaned, pushing, pushing, and luckily, grandma got there just in time to scream at me to catch him.

so he slid into my hands; i half pulled him out, and he was still attached by a snakish, veiny monstrosity to something left inside her, but i'd seen the movies, this is where they spanked the thing so the thing could breathe, but i wasn't doing that, not when this squashed elf face had its eyes open looking right at me and not when it gave a crooked spreading smile to me, just to me, the first smile that his mouth had ever made.

the cutest smile on earth.
and that's how i knew that he belonged to me, that he would mean everything to me and i would mean everything to him.

do you know why she named him akio?
she named him after my childhood playmate—she said she wanted him to be with me always.

my grandmother took one look at him and said,
wrathful deity.
why? my mother said. *he's not even crying.*
you'll see, said my grandmother.

so that's the first thing. that's the first real thing.
i'm sitting here in front of the computer, and it feels good to be finally telling the truth, telling whatever it is
that rises to the top.
it would be easier if you were here with me—if we could stay up all night talking. then i could watch your face, to see if you hated me for telling the raw truth. i would start with the story of my brother's birth, and if you still didn't hate me, i would trust you to say a little more.

i finally stop for a moment and look up, catching my face in the dark window. beyond my reflection, the red lights of the train station.

this could be the loneliest time—but you're with me,
i can feel you, just on the other side of the screen . . .
reading my deepest thoughts.
impossible, though.
i haven't posted one word. yet.

2. Chelsea

i came straight home from school, cranked the air conditioner, grabbed my computer, sank onto my bed. let me explain why i'm lying here in the icy dark and haven't written a word.

i'm not who you think i am.

i live in hollywood, but i'm far from melrose. you've mentioned that street, and you probably think of melrose the way i think of harajuku—a mix between heaven and oz.

but the big glittering blocks of melrose give way to smaller residential streets—bright red bungalows with yellow shiny roofs, yards with monkey trees and flamingo lawn ornaments . . . and those turn into broken, uneven sidewalks, one of the oldest neighborhoods in hollywood, unpretentious, somewhat seedy—and when you come to the little yellow house, the paint peeling, the grass overgrown, with a lawn mower rusting in the center of it—snap, my house.

i tried to see it through your eyes just now, i even pretended

that i had never walked in the door before—took a big whiff of the air—because what if we were one of those people whose house had a smell—like burnt eggs or steamed cabbage—god—
but it smelled okay. an herbal face wash smell still in the air from my shower. i noted the mess here and there, the clutter, the old coffee table with the glob of glitter glue that never came off.

not that i think you're obsessed with surface things. nothing has ever made me think that you would care if i turned out to not be the head of an elite loliclique.

school, though. you would hate it with every fiber of your being. unless we made up an alternate persona for you. turned you into a girl from harajuku, who had—i don't even know, and who would we be doing this for? not for you. the last thing you want to do is fit in. but i've thought about these things, i've thought about all of it nonstop. even when i'm on to something else, there you are again.

you and your brother.

† † †

so i'm lying here and i don't want to move. my room's a mess, dark, because i have black paper taped up over the windows with black tape. creepy, i know. bordering on overwrought emo, i know. or it would be if i had little emo geek friends over strumming little emo guitar bits while we pretend to get high on nighttime cold medicine. but no one comes here, and i put the paper up years ago because the journalists were looking in, getting their cigarette and coffee breath all over the window. now i just like it dark.

there's the distant buzz of a lawn mower. a barking dog. busy morning. nothing to hear in my quiet house but the hum of the air-conditioning.
nothing to see but the cracks in the ceiling. the familiar shape of the elephant. the tarantula.

memphis and i used to lie on my bed and watch the water stains and cracks form themselves into shapes . . . the elephant was mine, the tarantula his. memphis loved spiders. *chels, it's really there,* he said.

and it is, still, a fine network of cracks that reform themselves into the delicate outline of a perfect, lethal spider.

i begin counting the legs automatically. but my elephant—had she always been such an illusion? it doesn't matter, she's the last elephant in my room, all the others are shoved beneath a mess of old clothes on the shelf in back of my closet. i used to collect elephant pictures. it makes me feel like crying to think of them, not because i miss them, but just to think that i used to be so dumb—or so *something*. . . .

my body's heavy. my eyes are too, but i won't sleep in the afternoon, falling into dreams, the dark ones you have when you sleep on a sunny afternoon, i will not fall into them even though my eyes close, and cloaked in velvet darkness, i begin the descent—
i sit up straight, heart pumping.
i'm alive and awake.
and i owe you the truth—even if it turns out i'm not who you want me to be.

3. Miya

i was wrong to tell you that part first,
about akio being born.
i should have started by saying that my mother grabbed me one hot night and we escaped.

my mom and dad had been fighting all night and it was late and the window was open, but it just gave us a rectangle of still black air to look at. i was on the floor, making demented little drawings. i was trying to see how tiny i could draw and how many tiny figures i could cram on to one piece of paper.

out of nowhere, mom puts on lipstick, grabs me. dad suddenly springs into action, tries to stop us, tells mom she shouldn't take me. for once, i am rooting for her to win—and she does—and out we go into the black heat.

i didn't care about their fight. i felt light with excitement and had a flash that mom and i might never come back.

next thing: shimokitazawa, funky tokyo neighborhood.

winding, narrow streets, smoky coffee places, tiny bars, punk music stores. then mom steers us through an alley, and before i can really see where we are, she drags me through a dented metal door.

don't know how she found it—no numbers or sign.
we go down a few flights, the stairs lit by bare bulbs. burnt popcorn stings our noses. mom leans her back against the wall, fingers touching her forehead—
she recovers, smiling, waving away my concern—*the heat,* she says.

inside: tiny theater. we grab first-row seats, prop our feet on the low stage in front of the screen, and tilt our heads back. lights out.

my favorite miyazaki cartoon. gives you a lurch when it's over, like you've landed hard back in the normal world.

† † †

was after midnight when we got out. forgot the trains had stopped running. the night was dripping with wavy color, the overheated streets nearly empty. we turned onto an unknown street, searching for a taxi.

we were the only ones on the block, but pounding music and smoky plumes of pine incense trailed out of a high window. a beautiful man was standing in a doorway with a beautiful woman, whispering things to her that made her giggle. we both stood there with longing, watching them—

i used to have so much fun, mom said. my head was kind of resting on her shoulder—it was such a special night.
i will *have so much fun,* i thought.
and just as i was moving off into that dreamy fantasy, she said: *miya, i'm pregnant.*

† † †

we kept walking, kept looking for a taxi, passed a guy unloading crates of live pink fish from the side of a truck. one of the fish jumped up out of the crate and flopped at my feet, making me scream.

we were out there for almost an hour before i saw the first one.

the girl was camouflaged into the base of a tree.
like she would prefer not to be seen or had been placed there and warned not to leave. she cuddled her black purse to her chest. her eyes looked out at nothing, calm, almost regal. there was an ancient, wavering heat around her. she was like a vision from another century.

oh, them, my mother said.
them?
she gave a flick of her hand—toward a garbage can at the base of the bridge, and i jumped a little inside: *another one.*

they had the air of homeless people, of untouchables. i realized the whole landscape was studded with them.
they stood like ghosts or huddled against walls, clutching dolls. perfectly still, dark as crows, lovely as death—gothic lolitas. the scary ones, not the ones with expensive clothes and lace-trimmed parasols. i didn't know that's what they were called back then—i didn't know until years later

when matsu explained it all to me. all i knew was that they seemed to be made out of shadows.

i didn't feel safe until we came to a well-lit, open plaza, where a few couples were still walking.

† † †

we ended up in front of that statue—everyone calls it a fountain, near the mejii shrine, with a giant white puppy in it, fashioned by yoshitomo nara, a continual track of tears seeping from the puppy's eyes. and a smile on his face, as constant as his tears. he was standing in a crystal pool of his own tears.

hey, i just realized something. mom was staring at the sky. i waited, but she said nothing more. i stood on the fountain edge, looking into the dog's crying eyes.
his snoopyish nose sticks over the guardrail, and people always patted it for good luck, or they made wishes, so many wishes that it had been worn smooth and shiny. i stroked it absentmindedly, feeling so happy that i wasn't even sure if i wanted to wish for anything. the heat was still like a black

blanket, but it seemed softer than before.

maybe you could step in and splash around—my mother had an innocent devil expression.
nah, i said.
i bet you don't know the real story about the fountain, she said.
okay, here we go.
if you put in your most cherished possession and make a wish for someone else, she said, *it will definitely come true.*
i gave her a hard look.
it's the ***new jersey*** *version*, she said.

my mother was born in new jersey but had come to japan when she was young and has been here all her life. whenever she did or said something a little out of line with reality, she would blame it on new jersey.

i actually had the rock my mother had given me, from the beach, in my pocket. i'd grabbed it when we left the house because it was my most treasured possession. i thought about placing it in the fountain, for my mother's happiness. but she already was happy in that moment, she was so happy that it seemed like greed or bad luck to keep wishing for it.

† † †

years later.
i was fourteen.
on the way back to the train station, after my time with matsu, i stopped to rest for a moment. matsu's bag of clothes wasn't that heavy—it was more that i wasn't ready yet to get on the train and go back to my life.
it was gray and starting to rain, and everyone else was running for cover. the plaza was basically deserted.
i was sitting on the edge of that fountain again. my mother had been gone for a year. i had been at the morningstar foundation home for most of that time, and i was sitting on the edge of the fountain where we'd been so happy. the rain began to fall in sharp points, making tiny circles in the water of the fountain.

i've been hiding this dog story for so long, the dog is somehow part of me. dogs bury things and they sometimes dig them up again. this story about the money was one thing i wanted to leave buried, but i promised to tell you the things as they rise up.

i felt the weight of the money in my deepest jeans pocket pressed against my leg. i knew it was mine to spend. the night before, matsu had fixed me up on a date with a boy. she was on a date too, both of us wrapped in blankets, beneath the fireworks, with our dates.

with each illumination of the sky, i turned away from the boy's face and watched the birds flying from the trees, shattered black forms against the sky, terrified.

look at me, he said, in the heat of the passion i did not feel. in those moments, i made myself see shōnen, the one i had been saving myself for.

afterward, in her apartment, matsu yelled at me: *if you had told me you were a virgin, we could have gotten more!*

† † †

i found a comfort in the puppy's tears.
he had such a simple appearance, but i could feel his complicated soul.
i felt like climbing into the fountain and putting my arms

around his neck—
but i sat on the edge, squinting up at the sky, feeling the last of the afternoon sun on my cheeks before i caught the train back home.

4. Chelsea

when we were eleven, we were equal.
we each posted a sentence the first day of our blogs.
and the next day, another sentence. for two years.
but when memphis disappeared, i didn't post a word.
and the next day, not a word. and day by day,
the silence built, a silence that was much easier to keep than speaking.

i wrote nothing for three years.
now we are both sixteen, and in some ways,
closer than before,
and in others, more than a continent apart.

if i never have the guts to talk to you, if i never see you in my life, if we never hear each other's voice—

what will i have given to you?

5. Miya

the glass is cool against my forehead, and it's almost blue out there, a deepening indigo, swallowing everything. i remember when i was little and i'd wake so excited just before dawn, and how i'd watch the colors come back into the world. it terrifies me to think of never being able to go inside that forest again.

if you were here, we could run outside at the very first light and i'd show you the forest. it could be amazing. if you were here with me, i know we would be talking all night, unable to sleep, the things would pour out of us.

your brother's so quiet, you would say if you were here.
he was born that way, i would say. *but don't worry, it doesn't last long.*

akio didn't cry when he was put down in his crib, he didn't cry when he was wet or hungry. my mother didn't think it was a problem, and my father didn't think it was a problem. but i could see that it was all blocked up inside him . . .

and then one night, we were all awakened by akio's first hysterical scream.

† † †

if you were here, you might be squirming. you might be suddenly hungry, i wouldn't blame you, they hardly ever have any good food around here. you might even be thinking about those delicious *okonomiyaki* the american made the other afternoon. i don't know how she did it, she offered to help—and next thing, she was whipping up ingredients from our kitchen like a pro. i didn't taste them, actually, but they looked amazing—crisp and delicious, little vegetable pancakes.

but you might not be hungry. or you might be willing to wait—if i told you that akio is a part of me and everything starts with him.

by the time he was three weeks old, he cried like his heart was broken and screamed like he was being burned alive. when he was afraid, all the color literally drained from his face and made him look gray.

he was having such long bouts of crying that both my

parents were starting to look like zombies, so i tried to help out.
i was walking him around one night, and every time i would try to sit down with him, he would whimper. so up i'd go, to the point where my arms were aching and my back had knives and i was so tired, i had to stand leaning against a wall.

i stood just inside the kitchen, where the blue numbers on the digital clock glowed from the stove. i saw the uncanny depth in his eyes, almost as if he were telling the time.

i stood with my eyes closed for a moment, akio's warm heaviness in my arms. i must have dozed for one fraction of a second, because my eyes snapped open and i was shocked to still be in the kitchen, with the noise of the refrigerator and the harsh moon coming through the small window. i felt weary with resentment and happened to look down at akio. he was smiling up at me. i slid down the wall and knelt there looking at him, rocking him slightly. his expression was calm and ecstatic, his skin so pure and silky.

his entire hand curled around my finger like the tail of a sea horse. he was completely still, but he was looking up at me, and as i looked back, his face began to change. what i saw was so astonishing, i felt like i should run and wake mom and dad. but i was transfixed, it was like a show. his eyes were open, but he must have been dreaming.

no, it was more than a dream, the things that passed over his face. his expression was changing, delicately morphing. i was hardly breathing, kneeling there in the blue light and shadows, peering into his face. expressions flickered over his face like the gods were showing me a sacred movie that explained his complete essence. expressions way too mature for a baby or even a child, readjusting his features, deepening his eyes.

in this waking dream, akio's eyes were animated by fright, surprise, joy, thoughtful pondering, each lasting only a beat, smoothly shifting into the next. it was like watching him evolve within a transparent chrysalis. it was impossible to tell if i was seeing his future or he was reliving the things from the previous world.

it lasted only a few minutes, and then his eyes closed and his face relaxed and he slept in my arms. i looked out the window at the white moon. there was a warm peacefulness within me, but then a kind of truth began to sink in.

he'd been *somewhere* before he came here, and maybe he had once belonged to someone else.

† † †

but he came to be mine in eight million ways.

when i patted his tiny shoulder when he cried and i felt his tiny hand reach back and pat me back. when he brought me presents of glitter and pennies and rocks wrapped in paper scraps. when i fed him his bottle, when we played in the woods—i could nearly forget that there was a time when i existed without him.

† † †

he came to be mine, and if i don't get out of here tonight, i know that american's going to take him away.

6. Chelsea

i was hungry just now so i went to the fridge.
i knelt in front of it, eating spicy thai rice from the take-out place. cold.
then a hunk of cake. with my hands. mom would kill me. a big swill of flat ginseng cola.

then i go in memphis's room and i fall to my knees again.

7. Miya

twice, they tried to take him from me.
the first time was my own mother—on the day she didn't come back.
she packed him up like he was a picnic lunch,
setting out toward the beach with a look on her face that made me say—*i'll watch him for you, mom.*
sometimes i wish that i had just gone with her.

on the darkest nights, doubts skitter through my mind.

but when she didn't come back, it was more than guilt that bound me to my brother; he was the only person left to love.

my father was a ghost in a shell since the day my mother left us. even more remote when his mother died, only a few weeks later, after her second stroke.
he barely cooked for us, never held akio. he would bring strange things home from the store—a handful of turnips and some candied plums, a little rice—and i'd try to figure out a meal from it. dad took akio to the specialist, and on

that same afternoon—like he'd thought it through for weeks—dad gave me the news. he was going to put my brother in a home so the government could pay for his care.

we were sitting in the kitchen and i was watching huge greenish white moths fluttering around the light over the sink. *i won't leave him*, i said.

fine. my father's face was smooth, no emotion. *you'll go with him.*

no argument, no discussion.

less than a week later, dad put us in his silver subaru and drove the short distance to this place.

he was the worst communicator i ever met in my life.

i didn't believe dad could go through with it—and none of it felt real, until i woke up the next morning shaking with fear—the first time in my life to not wake in my own bed. the first time in my life to not have my forest just a few feet from the door.

but i could see it from the window.

and i had the shōnen books and my brother in bed with me.

i dressed my brother and fed him and carried him down to the forest that first morning. i decided to teach him things. i taught him about the elephant spirit inside the tree—but he discovered the spiders by himself.

† † †

his eyes lit up the first time he saw a spider—it walked up to him like a puppy.
it scurried behind him to hide when i tried to catch it, like akio was his god.
it's been three years of it, following him into the woods so he can find spiders and i can dream.

† † †

last week, we were hunting under rocks and up in the trees. akio was the one to find her, in a silver web between two tree branches, looking at us with her sharp spider eyes, breathing in the brackish air over the pond.

a bug flew onto her web, and she went into action.

only something went wrong—the line was too short and the bug got tangled in the web. she had to rip her little mummy bug out by force, destroying her web in the process.

it was time to leave, but akio wanted to stay and watch the action. he began to scream and he screamed and punched me and pulled my hair all the way up the hill to the home.

† † †

the next day, he dragged me back and pulled me into the woods and found the exact branch where the spider had found the fallen bug—and there she was again, getting ready to feast.

if you were here, we could easily teach you how to find a certain spider on a certain branch deep inside the woods. it looks like magic, but it's not.

i reach for a shōnen book—
shut my eyes—
should i take him away from the forest?
or wait, maybe i should ask: *how much time before someone tries to take him from me?*
which question first?

but i can't find my path in a book tonight, so i'm in front of my computer, leaning into my screen, and i still feel you as if you're just on the other side, waiting for me to post.
my heart is forcing me to talk.
it's not stories i need to tell, it's something else.
i don't even know what will come from this dark form that fills every part of me and has never been spoken to anyone.
time to let it out.

8. Chelsea

i'm on my brother's bed, under his blanket, head on his pillow, no blacked-out windows here—sun fills his room. there's a chalkboard on the far wall; the day we got it, i scrawled *i ♥ u,* in bright pink chalk. beneath it, in lime green, is the wavery heart that memphis drew. a few years ago, it hurt to look at it—i couldn't even come in this room—and now i'm curled up on his bed gazing at those two hearts.

9. Miya

i write to you until everything is out that wants to come out. i don't think about it, i don't even make a little wish, i click on the little red thing that says post. and send it all out.

† † †

looking out the window at the stars, thinking about my father.

i go into akio's room—to pack, to wake him, maybe—but he's not sleeping at all. he's standing on his bed, looking out his window too.

i sit at the edge of his bed.

miyathebook, he says, tumbling into my lap.

i open it up. . . .

10. Chelsea

when he was in the mood, my father was a great storyteller; at night, we'd all end up crowded on memphis's bed, pulled in by dad's stories, which always began like this:

a long time ago, there were spiders that ran sideways and ones that hopped. . . .

that's how they began when i was little, and he was still telling them the same way when memphis was little. my father spun his own web of words around us. he created a tight, unknowable world, and as i drifted off, i saw myself being woven inside it.

one night, in the middle of a story that had begun with one strand and wound into adventures so complicated that they made my heart race, memphis stood up straight in bed.

let's go there now!

whoa, said dad, holding his hand up like a traffic cop. *it's night,* he said. *we won't be able to see anything.*

so memphis ran into my room the very next morning and begged me to take him hunting for spiders.

† † †

my mother and i have built a fragile house. it's built around an escape plan and it's constructed of routines.
our quiet times of shopping, even the way we laugh, contain the pain of missing memphis.
our silent car rides of just me and mom contain all four of us screaming out memphis's favorite rap song.
loss is folded automatically into every joy; the secret to our perfect escape plan is: to never forget, and never go back to our old ways.

for years, we barely cooked—even the smells of certain foods used to make us fall apart. although she's been cooking lately—and the bigger the dinner, the more it feels like betrayal to enjoy what she's prepared.

but more than food, it's the dining room table itself, the sense of noise and light around that table—we haven't eaten there for so long. it's piled with bills and odd things. we eat in front of the tv, usually together. where would a new person sit? impossible to envision someone in memphis's room again, on the other side of my wall, unless it's my own brother knocking.

† † †

do you understand how many years i have looked at the spider on the ceiling in my room, looked at it as if my brother himself had crawled up inside it and never come out. i couldn't have people passing me in the hallway at night who didn't understand about spiders.

† † †

memphis was always the one to wake me in the morning, with a shout, a violent kick—or sometimes a soft pat on my cheek. sometimes he'd wake me with the intensity of his gaze. it was eerie to wake staring into his somber eyes—
his face would break into instant relief, as happy to see me as if it had been forever that he'd been waiting—we could finally start the day—even if it was some wretched early hour.
he was so alive that he almost always made me happy to be awake.

† † †

we had our favorite spot in the woods, in the park across from our house, behind the kiddie playground. mom would sit by the swings in the sun, and we would duck inside and pick up where our last game had left off.

the games i played with memphis were intricate, the rules inspired by the shōnen books.

each wet green leaf was a hiding warrior and each brown one a dead warrior and if a red leaf blew into the pond and began to spin in a cycle, it was a drowning warrior! we had to fish it out quick with a stick or all his energy would go and another rainbow warrior would bite the dust.

memphis knew that i could hear the little wishes of things.
which leaf?
that one.
how do we get the elephant out of the tree?
he looked at me rapt, dazzled. he believed every word with such a perfection of belief that i had to make everything i said worthy of hearing. even when i told him there was an elephant in the tree.
when he was listening to me, i didn't feel like i was lying

or pretending, i felt like i was creating the world.

we need to hug her, we need to drop a stone onto this pile, we need to do it one thousand times, that's what she says, can't you hear her?
and then the spell will be broken and she'll come out and give us a ride.

† † †

i was always ready to go into the woods with memphis—until the summer i turned twelve.

for a year i hung out with mariah and dylan and whenever i forced myself to go back with memphis, the woods seemed old and dull, the bugs were annoying. i was impatient to leave.

and i didn't drag myself there on that saturday morning in september when memphis woke me. it was one of the last days before school was starting. i was thirteen by then and looking forward to eighth grade, somewhat. i was getting everything i could out of the last days of summer, and i had stayed up all night online with mariah and our gang.

i was so tired and it was so dark, i was barely conscious when memphis came in. later it had the quality of a dream; i might have even believed it was a dream if i hadn't remembered his exact last words to me.

memphis came into my room, bounced on top of me and demanded that we go out—
he had his red coat on—
he came into my room saying he wanted to go hunt for spiders in the woods.
come on, chels, he said.
i said no, or nothing at all, turned and hugged my pillow.

† † †

i'm not ready to give up hope.
i'm not ready to give up my brother's room.

my answer to my mother will be no—but i'm still dreading telling her.
check my cell—three a.m. her time. way too early to call her.
i go online—i don't even know why, i barely expect you to post anything on the night of your father's funeral.

but you have written.

i shut my eyes.

you've written the longest entry of all time.

i almost don't want to see it. correction. i don't *deserve* to see it.

how could i read about your life after making such a clear choice—

and then i read your first words, and they are written directly to me.

i know you would never let me drown.

—my heart dives down to get you.

i race through it the first time, stabbed by the details, the connections between us so dense and interwoven, a forest springs up around me. and in the darkest, thickest part of these woods, you show me an ancient web, and there it is, trembling in the center, not a spider but your beating heart.

i turn away, and turn back, because there is nowhere else to turn.

i really get it now: you're in trouble.

i won't let you drown.
you need me—and your trust in me is complete.
i need you too.
my choice is yes—it's time to stop the world.

† † †

i go on my own blog, ready to spill.
i want to let it all flow, a river of ideas and feelings and questions—but there's no time for such luxury, not when you're suffering.
i had a brother, i tell you. *we were in this game together—just me and him creating the world, and three years ago, he disappeared. . . .*

i write just a little—enough to explain why i've been away. i tell you that i'm ready. and even as i say it, i feel like i am crossing over a line and will not be able to return to this in-between land again. even as i tell you yes, i feel myself being pulled back into the world of the living, the world i've tried so hard to escape.

i want you and your brother to be here, i tell you.

and then i press post.

and on my bed, in all my clothes, with the birds still chirping outside, i cry myself to sleep. i fall into the heaviest, longest sleep of my life, a sleep without dreams.

11. Miya

i read my brother the last page of the last shōnen book:

gothiclolita009 pricked herself with a thorn and showed him the quivering sphere of blood on the tip of her finger. are you sure you want to go deeper? *she said.* to be human is to bleed. . . .

he raised her hand to his lips and kissed the blood from her finger. if a drop of this is all that comes between us, i've never tasted anything sweeter . . . and yet, if we can't love as deeply without it, i've never known anything more bitter. . . .

it was time. the final moment had arrived, and his borrowed human form began to turn dreamlike and transparent—009 clung to him more tightly. my spirit says for you to stay in the crystal realm where you can serve so many others, but my heart insists that i must see you again, even in another form, no matter what the cost—even if only for an instant—

she looked at shōnen's face for the very last time, in the evening sunlight, a light that softened things and also made them clear.

all the hidden birds were singing, and shōnen pulled her close for one last embrace and—

i feel a pang, again, always—when i reach the end and come to the page that is torn out. i would give anything to know how this book really ends. i've been making up endings for years.

akio's watching me, awake and patient. i gaze at the ceiling, too tired to think of a fresh ending. i think about getting him into his pjs, brushing his teeth—or maybe now is when we're supposed to make our escape—
next thing, i wake with the sound of my own snores and akio's dirty feet in my face.

it's not yet sunrise. *i'll be back*, i whisper to akio, and he bursts awake, throwing his arms around my neck. *me go with you!*

but just as suddenly, he falls heavily back on the bed. i straighten things out, tuck the covers over him, and before even using the bathroom or brushing my own teeth, i run online, to see if you've written back.

PART NINE.

1. Chelsea

i rip a big black strip of paper off my window—
is it morning?
barely. dawn leaks into my room. today's the day.
time to get dressed.

† † †

in my closet.

i haven't been in this closet forever.

start putting together something for today. all my stuff looks like crap—i dig into the back—find this perfect skirt with underwire boning like the rafters of a ship, but it will continue to hang useless. i rescued dozens of pieces from mom; she wore some cool things in the eighties. i wore them a lot one year; they fit so well, i sometimes believed they were mine. this morning they have an emptiness, reminding me of the shells that certain insects leave behind.

memphis's clothes are here too.

† † †

we were awakened by the sound of sirens.
we all thought the entire fire and all the police and ambulances were all about memphis. and then we all thought he would be instantly found.
and then he wasn't.
it was one of the worst wildfires in los angeles history; it started at the hollywood foothills and ripped through sixty acres of the park.
i looked for memphis everywhere.
when i sat, i looked for the place he would have sat beside me.
when i lay in bed at night, i didn't sleep, i listened for him.
i lay in bed with his favorite toys. and then i don't know what happened to me, except that i thought i was dead, but now i have to admit that i'm alive.

† † †

i call my mother and i tell her what i already wrote you.
i tell her that i understand that it's time to bring life back.
for the first time, i thank her for doing all of this. for wanting to adopt both of you.
and for the first time, i ask if i can speak to you—but she says you spent most of the day in your room and then ran off into the woods before dinner.
i can't imagine what you're going through, or maybe i can.
i just hope you're okay.

2. Miya

do you realize that your blog has landed in my world like a bomb?

i read what you had to say—so short, so intense, each sentence a blow to my gut.

i feel sad and shocked for all you've been through with memphis. but also betrayed—you've been there all along—you knew the trouble i was in—and you didn't tell your mother to adopt us until now. and your mother—she's the *american*?

i go numb. maybe i should be celebrating, but i go numb. no need to run away now—or maybe now is the time to run, as fast as i can. i feel like decisions and fate have been ripped from my hands. the inside of my head feels fragile, like crowds have been screaming inside.

lie in the dark. room jumping with shadows. so tired and shattered, can't tell if my eyes are opened or closed. the house is starting to wake up, but i stay in my room.
let them think i'm sleeping up here. or praying.
in reality, frantic things are scrambling through my mind. i should grab akio—just grab him and get on the next train—or hide out in the forest—but that's insanity—try to force myself into calm, but adrenaline's pumping in me so hard i want to scream—i need to think, my head's turning my thoughts into a blended mess and i need out of here—and none of your words are sinking into my head—the only thing i know for sure is panic.

late in the day, i wrap myself in my black cape and fly

downstairs, into the industrial kitchen—the insides of my stomach are touching—opening the staff fridge—
always best to sneak from the staff fridge—and there it is-little wrapped stack of the precious *okonomiyaki,* stuff it into my bag—and i grab one of her american water bottles—and i'm running.

† † †

i didn't really mean for you to answer.
i didn't really understand that you were human.
i don't know if i can leave my home. i don't know anything right now but hard running.
i'm running away to nowhere. at the horizon, the dark blur of woods. but i head to the cliffs. i'm running so fast, i can taste the burn in my lungs. my heart in my ears.

i cut through to the break in the forest, where the ground is highest, and you can see the ocean far below. start scrambling down the cliffs, wind whipping my hair into my face, every step and every rock familiar—i could do this blind.
stopping at my mother's spot—on a jutting rock, the ocean right below me.

close enough to feel the spray of surf—high enough to tumble in.
—seeing what she saw—nothing on top of the ocean but the shifting silver and copper waves—but underneath, huge things and billions of them. anyone could slip from any one of these sharp rocks, no guardrail.
one more step and—
when she looked to the left, she would see the river, the train station—and rising up behind the town, mt. fuji. or did she see nothing—nothing left to live for, not even me and akio? i know she didn't fall.

i know she never meant to be found, but she was.

let me run to the beach now, seagulls flying in the last light of the day,
wind stinging my ankles with sand.
the noise of the surf is in everything.
a bird at the edge of the water, moving in fast starts, then stopping, leaving marks shaped like japanese letters, stamping the beach with unreadable stories.
the sky is eight brilliant hues, and it should look beautiful, but it doesn't.

i can't connect.

the ocean sends white froth over my toes, and i move straight into the loud, crashing sea—as i move in farther, i won't feel the cold or the wet because the rage in me will be so hard, and the crash of the surf will keep absorbing it and the more i scream the more i feel it building, waves of rage, and it won't matter if my screams can be heard, it'll only matter that i'm making them—loud enough to scream without being heard, i don't even know what words—sound, i make a sound, the sound feels torn from my throat, i can hear it even as it's swallowed by the waves. i hold the rock she gave me in my hand—*here,* screams the sound—*how could you?* i scream to her—*take it,* i scream to her—*i miss you so bad,* i scream to her—better to throw the rock into the sea, better to do it now than to let it go into a tiny pool of dog tears. but i can't leave it here, the ocean is too vast and sad.

3. Chelsea

i peel the whole sheet of black paper off, unlatch the window, slam on the frame to get it unstuck.

the air hits my face bitter and fresh, everything quiet except for a garbage truck rolling around the corner.
i see the sun, a fierce day-glo pink fire near the bottom of the sky.
the glittering sidewalk is clean of all debris—i suck in the air, nothing more to see.

† † †

i wish my father hadn't left us so quickly, running away, surfacing months later, in oregon—and then vermont—leaving both of us alone in this house.
my mother was awake at night, for as long as i can remember, waiting until she thought i was safely asleep, to cry. tear by tear, she cried a river i could never swim across. i wanted to run into her room and save her from her suffering. i was trapped on the other side, in my bed, with my fingers in my ears, feeling an ache that would not release. i felt too small to speak the truth. i could only send a message from my heart: *how can you feel so alone, when i'm still here?*

miya, tell my mother i miss her and can't wait to see her.

please tell her that i'm proud of her and we'll find a way to deal with everything new.

no, don't tell her anything. there are things you and i will tell only each other.
from now on, you and i will be in this together.

† † †

you put up his picture right after memphis disappeared. i couldn't stand to see the face of a newborn, or any child. and you were so obviously in love.
at first i hated you for having a brother.
white-hot hatred, in fact. sometimes my day would pass in a fog of pain, and i would go on and read you so i could hate even more.

but then you revealed a few things—that you were in a home, that your mom had died—i felt sad for you, but you never showed your pain, you spoke as if you were focused on other things. you kept posting beautiful pictures, and one day i realized i was actually hoping for pictures of your brother—actually looking for them—and when you wrote about him, even a sentence, i would be reading with tears streaming down my cheeks. he'd remind me so much of memphis.

as much as i'd hated you, i loved both of you again. i began to worry about your brother as much as i worried about you. i liked watching him grow, and without even meaning to, i looked eagerly for new pictures, just to see that everything was okay.

† † †

i got in the habit, about a year ago, of bringing my computer into the living room. we'd eat, watch tv, and i'd stay in there doing my homework while mom stared at the tube.

i logged on to your site, as usual.
but this one night—i went out to the bathroom or whatever, and when i came back, my mother was staring at your brother's picture.
how did you find this girl? she wanted to know.
i didn't want to tell her anything, i felt so invaded. it had actually been so long since i had found you, i'd almost

forgotten about using the address scrawled in the back of the shōnen book.

my mother tracked you down. she never had a question about it—and i had way too many. will you ever forgive me for being silent for so long?

† † †

maybe i will never stop this habit of talking to you in my mind. after the things you wrote last night, i know the size of each stone in your path.
i can close my eyes and feel the warm buzzing, be transported to the world inside your forest. more alive than the only woods i know, in the park by my house. i'm going there now, to find my brother.

† † †

the playground is deserted. i run toward the break in the dense black woods.
only those gifted with special powers will know how to find the way back in.

4. Miya

i didn't know the pond would be so beautiful, or how good it would feel to sink my feet in the water and breathe in the air, heavy with birdsong and spinning dragonflies.
and the scent of rain . . . i find my mother again in these woods—a memory i had forgotten—

we were in the woods, and the wind had suddenly lifted and fat drops had begun to fall. then torrents, loud as tribal drums. we ran for a tree that had branches like curtains. we watched the rain turn the forest dark and greener, drenching everything. a bird called through it, two notes against the darkness.
it was a green pigeon—its voice so deep and hollow, the sound of a *shakuhachi* flute.

i just realized! my mother said. *those are the same two notes—the same two notes as a japanese ambulance. not a* ***new jersey*** *ambulance.* she caught my eye to make sure i was listening, and then she did a clownish imitation of a new jersey ambulance that made both of us fall down with laughter. my mother and i were always falling down with laughter, when she wasn't depressed.

i suck in the bitter scent of the woods, with the tears—
i loved my father, but she was my heart.

5. Chelsea

i slip onto the little path,
with the sun at the level of my eyes.
when i get there, the early-morning woods are darker and muted; washes of birdsong, like underwater flutes. there's an excitement in the air, and it's cooler than usual.

the rock's cold and heavier than it looks. it all comes back to me, that search for the perfect stone, how each had its own personality and own special part to play in the elephant game. i remember how memphis would search so seriously for the perfect rock, sometimes whispering to them, sometimes inhaling their essence like he was seeking an elusive perfume—but when he was convinced it was the right one, he'd call out *GOT IT* so triumphantly—because we never just put any rock at the base of the elephant tree.
i feel the icy smoothness of the stone against my cheek—

and i find the elephant tree—touching the gray, gnarled bark, tracing the familiar grooves.
when i was little, i knew in the pit of my stomach how exciting it would be when we'd add the thousandth stone to the pile at her base and she would at last be free.
i saw the same look on memphis's face when i told him the story my mother had once taught me and that her mother had once taught her.

6. Miya

i never could feel her heartbeat inside this tree. but i hug her now, her bark rough against my cheek.
when i was sad, my mother used to tell me to be like an elephant and vanish inside a tree.
i kept asking what she meant, so she took me to the woods to show me the elephant inside this tree. all i saw was a tree with one branch growing to the sky and the other growing out sideways to the pond.

luckily, grandma came and told a better story—she said that it was true, there was an elephant who had been in this forest a long time ago, but she had started out as a human,

and she wasn't actually that sad—in fact, she was the happiest girl alive—and her hair was made of rainbow-tinted leaves and her skin shone in rare and transparent colors—and she was so happy that she made all the other humans—and even the butterflies and birds—look tired and gray.
so one day, an old forest witch snapped her up and turned her into a giant gray hairy elephant, but she was *still* too happy, and so she forced the elephant into the tree. the only time her beauty was allowed to bloom was when the leaves of the tree turned brilliant colors in the fall.

and so my grandmother and i would come each day and give the elephant tree a hug, and then we put the stones there because we wanted to set her free.
and i used to wonder who would come out first—my mom's sad elephant or my grandma's happy one?
be happy, i whisper, leaving the rock mom gave me at the base of the tree.

7. Chelsea

i pick up a rock from the base of the tree and whisper my brother's name.

add my rock to the pile, grab fistfuls of the rocks and hold them to my face. all of them were touched by him.
i feel a crushing sadness, like it's all been pulled away from me. it makes me so sad that there are things that can never go back again, that you will never get to see exactly the same again.

i sit here in the leaves, feeling the shock of being in this world alone.
i feel how much i miss the stories we made together in the woods.
i let it settle into me.

memphis, i say again, his name in my throat, at once the most beautiful and saddest word in the world—*where are you?*

8. Miya

the white flowers on the pond grow brighter, draining the last bit of light from the sky. i can push the tears back, but i can't keep back my love for this forest.
at sunset, the cricket chorus pricks through the heat, sparkles race across the water. all the hidden birds sing, and

their music is so eerie. until the sun sets, they sing here and there, never together, and always at this time they join together. it's so different and sad when they raise their voices together in this last song of the day. the deepest sound in the chorus is the green pigeon.
when i was roaming around on the internet once, i found this corny site called "rare sounds of the japanese forest." they had every sound alphabetized, every bug and bird. my favorite thing i ever posted on my blog was the mp3 of the green dove. i felt like i was sending you the whole forest.

† † †

and there it is, a flash of green—the green birds are so hidden, you can see only glimpses of their special green when they fly from the woods back toward the ocean at night. and suddenly, my heart feels painfully attached to it—what if it's the last time i see a green dove, and i can only listen to their haunting notes on the computer, again and again?

how can i leave all of this? it would almost be like leaving my body, it's all in my blood, it's like leaving god.

i have this wild urge to take all of it with me. i start running through the darkening forest, touching trees, feeling my heart breaking open—
running to my special spot—
be there, be there. my heart is in my throat.
i go beyond the pond and kneel in a field of moonlit leaves. i look only at the leaves, and it's so utterly silent, i feel the same sort of silence inside.
god, i begin—
the tears come.
god—

i gaze at the leaves and the world shifts. the puddled shadow side of the leaves and the silvered bright side of the leaves merge like an optical illusion, and you can't tell if they're leaves anymore. i feel only the dark and shimmering aliveness of the woods, and the feeling is so deep, it puts me to sleep right there in the leaves—*stay with me.*

9. Chelsea

come back to me. i run until i'm almost in the center of the woods—*come back to me, i know you're here*—and my legs get caught in the sharp, pricking bushes. i have to kneel to get myself free—but he's nowhere, and i hate this sunshine, hate this day, this life. and i really, really hate these woods. i can barely remember what it was like to spend a second inside this wretched place—and i'm wiping snot and i'm trying to pull free without ripping the thin cotton of this tank top—and a dash of light signals between the low branches, a quick flicker.

i move closer, my jeans pinching my stomach, and there it is, catching the light: the one strand—the kind that can always be found—of a web expired or just begun, the sun gilding it with trembling prisms of color that you can see only when you move close, and when you do, the colors shift, now green, now violet, quivering like the after-note on a plucked guitar string. when you move away, the strand is invisible—

not a thing you would think about for one other second in your life—

and if this is a sign from memphis—it echoes inside me, making me lonelier than before, softening my eyes with tears—

i still can't feel you, i beg. *are you mad at me? i said they could come.* i lower my voice to just below a whisper, my eyes squeezed shut. *just give me a sign that i'm not betraying you, that it's okay to bring them here.*

my cell's ringing.

10. Miya

look! i say, when i awaken. but the light's shifted and the leaves are ordinary again—and i'm talking to a tree. i'm cold and still wet from the ocean. i haven't slept long—
the sound of twigs and branches snapping—
your mother.
hey, she says, casual, friendly.
i turn away, embarrassed.
she starts to sit and then asks, *can i?*
i love these—she's touching the tops of those weird magenta flowers that poke through the fluorescent moss.
miya, she starts—ducking her head. shy. nervous.
i talked to chelsea—she leans forward.
i nod. for no reason, my eyes are filling with tears.
do you think you might like—she's so hesitant—

then she blurts out what's really on her mind: *do you think you might like to come live with us—you and akio?*
i feel a soft relief sweep through me.
i think i might, i say.

we should call chels—she's already digging in her bag, can hardly hide her excitement. then—*whoops, i left it in the house again. . . .*

11. Chelsea

my cell is ringing, and what the hell, i pick it up.
no one there. i'm about to click off, but then i hear breathing.
well, not quite breathing.
stifled giggles.
who's there? i demand, trying to sound imperious but barely keeping the joy out of my voice.

i'm pressing the phone to my ear, listening hard,
but i don't need another sign.

i'm awake.

i'm awake and i'm in the woods
with the california sunshine falling through the trees and a kid on the other side of the world giggling in my ear, and my heart's slamming.

for the first time in years, i feel like i'm about to jump straight off a mountain into the center of the action:
and i can see us.

i can see us here, in these woods, playing. i can see you and me chasing after akio—alive and strangely awake, in a world where all memphis has left behind of himself is rainbows everywhere.

12. Miya

she's so nervous, she's speaking half in english and half in japanese, and she keeps looking like she's on the verge of grabbing me in a giant hug.
then she takes her sweater off her shoulders and wraps me in it, that same sweater from her room. what really gets to me is her awkward way.
i didn't realize how shy she was, or how much she wanted us.

we're walking toward the cold white lights of the morning-star foundation, and that's one sight i won't mind leaving.
oh, look, she says—and we both see the moon rising quickly behind mt. fuji, so fast that in seconds it moves from just the rim to a big fat moon above the mountain.

i can't seem to move, looking at the moon above mt. fuji, the mountain taking up so much of the sky with its odd, flat top.
i never even touched this mountain.

† † †

she couldn't know—how could she know—all that's within me.
but maybe she does—she touches my shoulder lightly and says, *i'll see you inside?*
she follows the path of cold moonlight and disappears inside the house.

i don't know how long i'm out there,
memorizing the outline of the mountain as if it were something i could pack up and take with me.
there's a chilly breeze sending smells from the kitchen
out to me,

baking smells, noise and clatter—and i'm walking back, up the hill, thinking about what it will be like when i first see you.

i might look shy. i might even look away, or take just one tiny step toward you, but the truth is, one more step and—
i'm flying—
i'm flying now—
up the hill and into the house—
grabbing akio in a hug that makes him squeal—
then taking the stairs, almost falling as i run—
heading to my room so i can talk to you—so we can keep it going, the story that started from the time we were born, that's turning out to be real.

THANK YOU
for the refuge, yaddo.
for the pure love, alex & hailey.
for holding the truth as precious and not accepting anything less, my editor, ginee seo.
for the many hours of reading and insightful input: gillian Farrell; laurie oliver; lea moore; bob mecoy; my agent, jodi reamer; and of course, ginee.
for the design, michael mccartney.
for his playful essence and inspiration, and the permission to use the photograph of his puppy, yoshitomo nara, and to the kind tomoko omori and tomio koyama gallery.

for working with me so generously and offering uncanny interpretations of the characters, yoshie sunada, emily cole, tom kitahara,
shih sheng hung, beth cole, ali cole, sarah cole, janice jaime, kaori ibuki, joyce cheung,
nanako-chan, orion (you're the man), and milo (ditto).

for writing to me 100 years ago, emili kusunoki aka the talented EMYLI.
for going all the way to tokyo to photograph the girl on page 69, julia rose.
for kindly contributing his photograph on page 101, masayuki takaku (his work can be found on flickr).

for efforts and support, anna, tamar, josh, doug, shamsi, violet, viva, mizuyo aburano, ulli gruber, vivian welton, carmen yuen and her gothic lolita blog, lawrence ripsher, gideon davidson, and marcus beard, and for my dad, for charlie the spider tales.

for being a perfect runaway twin at a 2003 shoot in woodstock, ny:
akira joseph shimizu.

for 2004 shoot, writershouse, manhattan:
mcs: abner, michael, amy, jodi
shoot assistant: kristy parton
stylist: jannah
makeup: lindsay hile
costume: lisa metropolis & bryan viper
fashions: alise marie & willow

for the many talented actors who recreated harajuku scenes and the l.a. cosplay, including: morgan welton, michelle altunis, jean goto, calvin vu, jeffrellony salomon, foisol khan, dana corral, len shigemoto, lena chen, jordan carl, jassica liu,
luke anable, john passantino, frank lin, adrienne smith, jason smircich, and akira dudley. if they're not in the book, find tons of outtakes and extras online:

http://profile.myspace.com/gothiclolita009
www.youtube.com/user/gothiclolita009

for helping me to hear japan, midori iwashita, sawako, yoko kanno, and joe hisaishi.
to see: yuken teruya, and misaki kawai.
to know: yoko ono, yoshikichi furui, kenji miyazawa, banana yoshimoto, and hayao miyazaki-san.
and 1,000 more.

Acknowledgments